Midsummer Night's Dream

Text of the First Quarto 1600

Characters

Theseus	Duke of Athens
Hippolyta	Queen of the Amazons, betrothed to him
Lysander	⎱ young men in love with Hermia
Demetrius	⎰
Hermia	in love with Lysander
Helena	in love with Demetrius
Egeus	Hermia's father
Philostrate	Master of Festivities for Theseus
Oberon	King of the Fairies
Titania	Queen of the Fairies
Fairy	serving Titania
Puck	goblin spirit, Oberon's jester
Peaseblossom	
Cobweb	⎱ elves serving Titania
Moth	⎰
Mustardseed	
Peter Quince	a carpenter, *Prologue*
Nick Bottom	a weaver, *Pyramus*
Francis Flute	a tailor, *Thisbe*
Tom Snout	a seller of pots and pans, *Wall*
Snug	a woodworker, *Lion*
Robin Starveling	a chimney-sweep, *Moonshine/Thisbe's mother*

Other fairies with Titania, goblins with Oberon

Civic officials, attendants, servants

In a cloudless blue sky of a midsummer morning, the sun is radiant over ancient Athens, the majestic stone columns of the Parthenon standing white and tall among the buildings high on the Acropolis which overlooks the city below, its wide streets bustling with people going about their daily routines: farmers in from the country to sell their meat and vegetables at market; burly artisans hawking their pottery and metal wares; robed philosophers in the shade of trees addressing young students seated on the ground at their feet; dust-covered sculptors chipping, chiseling and polishing their marble and granite creations; impassioned politicians on the steps of the temples, debating hotly; costumed actors in the open amphitheaters rehearsing their dramas, passersby occasionally stopping to view the sometimes tragic, sometimes comic but always entertaining performers.

Near the center of the city, in the public square lined on each side with towering stone sculptures of the pantheon—the gods and goddesses of Greek legend and myth—the largest crowds have assembled, for heralds wearing the gold sandals, crimson-red robes and gold-winged helmets of Theseus, Duke of Athens, are proclaiming the news that their illustrious lord, commander of all the Empire, slayer of the Minotaur at Crete and vanquisher of the rapacious Periphetes, has returned victorious from his campaign in the east against the Amazons, the race of warrior women who for centuries have lived and flourished without the society of men.

But happily for all, upon the defeat of her armies, Hippolyta, Queen of the Amazons, has consented to become the wife of noble Theseus, the marriage to take place in the upcoming week, with much feasting and many festivities in store for citizens both young and old. Most especially welcome are those who will attend the forest promenade in the Cerean Woods just outside the city, at midnight on the evening before the Duke's nuptial celebration.

Jubilant, the crowd erupts in a resounding cheer, because Theseus has for so long remained unmarried and without an heir that this announcement has brought great relief along with heartfelt joy. The Duke is at last going to take a bride, and a royal one at that!

*

Assuring them he won't be long, Theseus orders the solemn-faced civic officials who have come to see him this morning, to wait on the terrace with his entourage of attendants and servants while he goes down the low steps and starts across his magnificent palace courtyard: a rectangle of crushed quartz framing a length of lush, green lawn, at either end of which are spectacular white-marble water fountains depicting Poseidon, god of the sea, trident raised above his bearded head and torso as numerous dolphins frolic in the carved stone waves around his fish-shaped lower body.

Only Philostrate, the Duke's harried Master of Festivities, dares to follow Theseus into the courtyard. A stack of scrolls balanced precariously in his arms, he hurries to keep up with the quickly striding Duke, pleading for His Grace to take a moment and discuss the growing number of weighty matters requiring his urgent attention.

But business is the furthest thing from the Duke's mind right now. He's intent on speaking with Hippolyta, his bride-to-be, who in a sleeveless gold tunic is teaching a group of teenage girls how to use the bow and arrow. Self-conscious giggles alternating with frustrated groans and mild curses, the first-time archers, in white knee-length tunics, try hard to keep their wayward arrows from hitting the servants further down the lawn, whose task it is to hold tight the broad white sheet, dotted in the center with a red triangle, that serves as their target.

Sensing the girls' frustration, Hippolyta patiently tells them to lower their bows and watch while she reviews, then demonstrates, the techniques of proper shooting. She pulls an arrow from the leather quiver on her back, fits it easily onto the bowstring, lifts, aims and lets go with an arrow that in the blink of an eye has left a small hole in the very center of the red triangle through which it has just passed, the girls murmuring in astonishment to see a woman shoot with the skill of a man.

Theseus nods approvingly as he comes to stand with his betrothed. "Now, fair Hippolyta, our wedding day draws quickly near. Though it is no more than four happy days until the new moon is upon us," he protests, "yet I can't but feel this old one is taking her own sweet time to fade—she toys with my anticipation like a withering widow who stubbornly withholds her inheritance from an overly impetuous heir."

"Four days will steep themselves in night," says Hippolyta, watching as the girls practice doing what she has just shown them, their performance noticeably improved now that Theseus is here. "Four nights will quickly dream away the time," she assures him, "till the new moon, a silver bow bent in the night sky, bears witness to our solemn and most wished-for vows."

Theseus gives her a questioning look: her words, though loving enough, seem forced—rather more what she knows he wants to hear, than what she would like to say. Nonetheless, he turns to his Master of Festivities with great enthusiasm. "Go, Philostrate! Rouse the youth of Athens to merriment and mirth. Bring the spirit of gaiety to life in our fair city. Drive melancholy to the funeral grounds—sadness and gloom are not welcome here at our celebration."

Philostrate holds up his armful of scrolls in earnest appeal, but Theseus only shakes his head and turns back to Hippolyta. Considering himself dismissed, Philostrate bows to the Duke and makes his way back through the courtyard and up the steps to the terrace where members of the civic delegation converge upon him and, in great consternation, demand to know what is going on…

Since her young archers are now able to reach the white sheet with their arrows, Hippolyta has the servants move ten paces back. The girls let out a collective groan—just when they thought they were doing so well!

"—I wooed thee with my sword, Hippolyta," Theseus says coming up behind her, "I won thy love doing thee injuries." He moves closer and places his hands tenderly on her shoulders; she continues watching the girls. "But I will marry you in a much different manner," he promises, his mouth close to her hair, "in pomp and splendor, in festivity and celebration—"

"Happy be Theseus, our noble Duke," a voice calls from across the courtyard.

Theseus turns to see a balding, bearded man in pale-blue robes charging forward, pulling two teenage boys along with him: one tall, dark and defiant looking, his cheek bones high, his pointed chin showing several days' growth of beard, while the other is fair-haired, finer in his features, with the air of maturity about him that parents of girls take to instantly, parents of boys urge their sons to emulate.

"Thanks, good Egeus," Theseus says as the man approaches. "What news with thee on this fine day?"

But Egeus dispenses with pleasantries and gets right to the point. "Greatly perturbed come I, my lord, with complaint against my daughter, Hermia." He notices both boys looking over at Hippolyta and the girls shooting arrows: one of them is the daughter in question, Hermia. The prettiest of the girls, though also the shortest, she lowers her bow and steps back from the shooting line, a worried look on her face...

"Step forward, Demetrius," Egeus has instructed the fair-haired boy, and he obeys promptly, presenting himself to the Duke with a respectful bow. Egeus regards the young man and smiles. "My noble lord, *this* man has my consent to marry the girl—" An annoyed frown replacing the smile, he motions to the dark-haired boy. "Step forward, Lysander." His eyes on Hermia, who is coming toward them now, Lysander doesn't hear: Egeus grabs him roughly and shoves him before Theseus. "—But, my gracious Duke, *this* man has bewitched her into thinking she loves him. You, *you* Lysander," Egeus points an accusing finger, "you've given her poetry and exchanged intimate keepsakes with this child of mine. At night, by the light of the moon, you've even crept up to her window and poured out your desires in wistful sad songs, and filled her head with wild fantasies by pressing upon her choice locks of your hair, rings, jewelry, baubles, trinkets, knickknacks, flowers, candies—*all* designed, in their sly way, to overwhelm the affections of a silly and inexperienced young girl—"

He breaks off, aware that Hermia has come up and taken a place beside Lysander. Still holding her bow, she glances coldly at her father, but Egeus only sneers and continues his bitter harangue.

"With cunning and deceit you have stolen my daughter's heart," he rails at Lysander, "and turned her obedience, which is due to me, to stubborn resistance against everything and anything I happen to say or feel! And, my gracious Duke, if it be the case that she will not, here in your presence, consent to marry Demetrius, then I beg the ancient privilege of Athens: that as she belongs to me, I may deal with her as I see fit—which will be either to marry this gentleman," he indicates Demetrius, "—or be put to death, according to the laws laid down expressly for such cases."

Theseus meets Egeus's eyes for a moment then looks to his daughter. "What do you say to this, Hermia?—Consider carefully, fair maid, for, to you your father should be as a god, your beauty what he fashioned for the world to behold—to whom you are but as a form modeled by him and bearing his name. Hence it is within his power to let his creation be, or alter it, if he so chooses. Demetrius is a worthy gentleman."

"So is Lysander."

"In himself he is. But in this case, knowing he is your father's choice, Demetrius must be held the worthier."

"I wish my father looked but with my eyes."

"No, it is you who must with his judgment look."

"I beseech your Grace to pardon me. I know not by what power I am made bold, nor how it may be received that I should dare to plead my case here in your noble presence, but I beg to know the worst that may befall me if I refuse to wed Demetrius."

"You will be put to death," Theseus replies bluntly, "or forced to give up forever the society of men." Hermia turns her eyes toward Hippolyta and the girls doing their archery. A cheer has gone up: several arrows have made it through the hole in the target sheet. "Therefore," Theseus continues, "it is best you question these feelings of yours, fair Hermia. Remember that you are still young and apt to be impetuous. In deciding whether or not to accept your father's choice, picture yourself wearing a nun's robes for the rest of your life, childless and alone within hallowed cloister walls, nightly chanting sad hymns to the cold, white moon. Blessed many times over are those who devote their lives to maidenhood, of course, but happier on this earth is the rose picked in ripe beauty, than that which, never plucked, withers away among thorns."

"So I will grow, so live, so die," she answers proudly, "before I will ever let my father decide on a husband for me."

Theseus takes in her reply then puts on a judicious frown. "Take time to think about this, Hermia, and at the shining of the next full moon—the day my love and I will be joined together in the bonds of matrimony—on that day either prepare to die for opposing your father's will, or wed Demetrius as he would like you to. Or, take the vow of chastity, denying yourself forever the joy of being a wife, and lead, forever, a holy but unmarried life."

"Think what you are doing, sweet Hermia," Demetrius pleads. "And Lysander, give up your unreasonable claim to what is rightly mine."

"You have her father's love, Demetrius. Let me have Hermia's." He flashes an insolent grin. "Marry *him*, why don't you—"

"Scornful Lysander!" Egeus erupts, "true he has my love. And what is mine, that love shall give to him: as she is mine, all my rights to what I own I here bestow on Demetrius."

"Your Grace," Lysander protests, "I come from a family as good as his, as well esteemed in this our city. My love is the greater, and my character is in every way equal to his, if it's not in some ways better. And—most important of all—beauteous Hermia is in love with me. Why should I not pursue my right to her hand in marriage? Demetrius—I'll say it to his face—wooed Nedar's daughter, Helena, and won her heart, and she, sweet girl, is desperate for the love of this deceiving and unfaithful man."

"I must confess that I have heard as much," Theseus muses, "and meant to speak with Demetrius about the girl. But being busy with affairs myself, it must have slipped my mind. So come along,

Demetrius, we'll talk the matter over now—and you as well, Egeus. I need to speak with you upon this matter also. As for you, fair Hermia, prepare yourself to accept your father's decision or comply with the law of Athens—over which even I cannot rule: to face your death, or take the vow of single life."

The matter done with, he walks over to Hippolyta. "My love, how are you..."

Hippolyta smiles but does not answer because Philostrate has returned, though without the scrolls this time.

"My Lord, we are waiting upon you," he says insistently, gesturing toward the terrace where the disgruntled civic officials are huddled in conference.

Theseus nods that he will go. "Come along, Egeus," he calls over, "I must make use of your services in these nuptial preparations, and help resolve this matter that concerns you so."

Without acknowledging his daughter, Egeus marches off, bringing Demetrius with him. They fall in behind the Duke and head toward the terrace.

Alone with Lysander now, Hermia looks down at her bow, deep in thought as she plucks idly at the string.

"What's wrong, my love, that your face grows so pale?" He runs a tender finger down her cheek.

"This edict of the Duke's perhaps has drained them of their color," she replies, "though I could drown my face in teeming tears with the tempest that torments me."

"I know," Lysander says and takes her hands in his, "in all I've read or heard, the course of true love never did run smooth. Through difference in family standing—"

"It's wrong when such a noble thing as love is reduced to this!"

"—or else some difference in age—" Lysander continues to explain.

"I'll not be treated like a child!"

"—or it was up to one's friends—"

"It's unjust having one's love taken away!"

"—or if the choice was agreeable to all, then war, death or illness found a way to come between true love, making it no more than a fleeting sound, swift as a passing shadow, short as a dream and brief as lightning which floods heaven and earth with radiance one minute, but the next—before one shouts 'Behold!'—the jaws of darkness devour it, and precious love is ruined."

Hermia leans her head on Lysander's chest. "If true love has ever been thwarted thus," she says sadly, "perhaps it shows what the future holds for us." She pulls her head away and looks up at him. "So let us learn patience in our adversity, see it as a burden that lovers must bear, as much a part of love as thoughts and dreams and sighs, as wishes, prayers and tears…"

"Yes, my love…" Lysander puts his arms around her and stares ahead, reflecting, until a thought strikes him. "—Therefore hear me. I have an aunt, a childless widow of considerable wealth who treats me like the son she never had. Her house is a mile from the city, we can be married there, for the reach of Athenian law goes not that far. If you do love me as you say, steal away from your father's house tomorrow night and I will meet you by the Cerean Wood—the forest where once with you and Helena I went one afternoon last spring."

"Dear Lysander," Hermia cries, overjoyed, "I swear to you by Cupid's strongest bow, by his finest gold arrow, in the name of Venus's chariot-bearing doves, by that which joins kindred souls and prospers loves—and by that fire into which the Queen of Carthage Dido leapt when Aeneas's departing sail was seen. —By all the vows men have broken, more numerous than those ever women have spoken—in that very place you have just told me, tomorrow I promise I will meet with thee."

"Keep your word, my love," he says and holds her close—but suddenly pulls away when a young woman comes down from the terrace and approaches them. A tall, gangling girl, cute rather than pretty, her face wears a distressed look.

"Fair Helena!" Hermia calls, "what brings you here?"

"You call me fair?" she demands and comes to stand with the lovers. "Take back the 'fair,'" she says despairingly. "Demetrius loves your 'fair': how lucky to be found 'fair.' He raves your eyes are like two shining stars, your breath the sweetest air, sweeter than the lark to shepherd's ear when wheat is still green, when spring buds first appear." She sulks and glances down at her hands, tears welling up in her eyes. "Love-fever is catching. If only it would catch me! What you have, Hermia, I would catch happily, my ear catch the sound of your voice, my eye the look of your eye, my tongue catch your tongue's sweet words. I would give anything in this world, except Demetrius, if I could but become like you." She clutches at Hermia's tunic. "Teach me to look like you," she pleads, "instruct me in that art with which you hasten the beating of dear Demetrius's heart."

"I frown at him yet he loves me still," Hermia defends herself.

"O that those frowns would teach my smiles such skill."

"I curse him yet he offers me his love."

"If only my prayers could such affection move!"

"The more I hate, the more he pursues me."

"The more I pursue him, the more he hates me."

"His foolishness, Helen, is no fault of mine."

"No fault but your beauty—if only that fault were mine!"

"Worry no longer. He no more shall see my face." Helena throws her a questioning look. "Lysander and myself will fly this place. Before I did ever Lysander see, Athens seemed like a paradise to me. But now what good in my love does dwell, when it has turned this heaven into a hell?"

"Helen," Lysander continues to explain, "to you our plans we will unfold. Tomorrow night when the silver moon has risen, and pearls of dew on the grassy fields glisten—the time when lovers' flights by shadows are concealed—through Athens' gates the two of us intend to steal."

"And in the wood," Hermia says, "where you and I on flowery banks beside the brook would lie, talking heart-to-heart of confidences sweet, there Lysander and myself have agreed to meet, and then from Athens turn away our eyes, to seek new friends and start new lives together. Farewell, true friend. Say your prayers for us, and good luck grant you your beloved Demetrius." She turns to Lysander. "Keep your word, my dearest love. We must starve ourselves of each other's sight until tomorrow, sometime after midnight."

"I will, my Hermia." She hands him her bow and quiver of arrows, kisses him on the cheek and then leaves. After she is gone, Lysander turns to Helena. "Helena, adieu. As you for him, may Demetrius feel toward you." He passes her the bow and arrows, and departs.

"How much happier some than others can be," she murmurs, watching the servants gathering arrows off the grass and rolling up the target sheet now that Hippolyta and her archers are gone "Throughout Athens I am thought as fair as she, but what does that matter if Demetrius thinks not so? He refuses to know what all except him do know. And as he mistakenly dotes on Hermia's eyes, so I do grow more admiring of all his qualities. Things badly out of key, Love can change to harmony: Love looks not with the eyes, but with the mind, and therein lies the reason Cupid's aim so oft' is blind. Nor does Love's mind with any judgment behave—instead with heedless haste it becomes enslaved. Therefore Love for a child is taken, since, in choosing, we so oft are mistaken. As mischievous boys will lie in their games, Love, without a thought, does just the same. For before Demetrius ever looked in Hermia's eyes, he hailed down loving oaths that he was only mine. And when this hail, some heat from Hermia felt, so he dissolved, and all his showering oaths did melt. I will go tell him of fair Hermia's flight—then to the wood will he pursue her tomorrow night, and for this knowledge to him conveyed, the thanks I earn will be more than the price I have paid. In doing this I will soothe the pain of losing his love by winning it back again!"

The last servant in the courtyard comes to collect the bow and arrows. Helena hands them over then gazes across the now empty lawn, the only sound coming from the jets of water gushing in the majestic fountains of Neptune at either end of the courtyard....

With auditions set to begin in the open-air amphitheater along one of Athens's busiest streets, there is much commotion and frantic activity as numerous troupes of actors scramble to finish their rehearsals: toward the rear of the stage, in front of the towering stone columns, a dozen bearded and well muscled men wearing scanty pieces of cloth around their loins, hold flaming tongs up to their mouths and breath fire on a fair-haired young man, in a loin-cloth as well, who continually breaks off strumming his lyre to wave it at the men breathing fire, whether as part of the play or for real it is hard to tell.

Further forward a crowd of voluptuous but drunken women encircles another budding Orpheus, whose beautiful singing can only keep them at bay so long before one of the women comes up from behind and gags him with a strip of purple cloth. Unable to sing, he watches in horror as the women close in with long-nailed fingers and pretend to scratch and claw him to death.

Off to one side, three women in flowing yellow gowns—similarly yellow ribbons trailing back from their auburn hair—dance in intricate patterns around a white-bearded old man whose booming voice reaches the upper levels of the curved row seats where Philostrate and Egeus, along with a handful of civic officials, are having a heated discussion about something.

"There are no answers, only questions!" the old man cries to a small crowd of spectators who have drifted in from the street.

Ignoring him, their concentration more focused on what one of their troupe has brought to eat and drink, six working men are laughing and lolling about the steps leading up to the stage, their whistling and rude catcalls drawing stern stares from the actors on stage. A shambling lot, not so much uncouth as unlearned, a howling guffaw from one of their members draws the ire of the young man on the lyre, who has suffered at the hands of the men breathing fire. Someone went too close with his flame and the young man's magnificent mane of golden hair has been reduced on one side to no more than a charred patch: a smoking remnant of its former glory.

Sensing trouble, Philostrate leaps to his feet in the upper seats and announces the auditions are about to get underway. He comes down the stairs quickly and hurries onto the stage, clapping his hands as he orders the troupe of drunken women to keep their places, while everyone else is to sit in the lower seats and patiently wait their turn.

The workmen mocking the young man with the smoking hair, Philostrate glares darkly and issues a stern warning to a man with the workmen whom he addresses as "Quince." The leader of the group, Quince realizes it would be wise for his troupe to wait elsewhere, so he herds them out toward the street, each one throwing winks and kisses at the voluptuous drunken women, who, busy refilling their goblets with wine, could apparently care less.

Once outside the amphitheater, Quince has his actors gather round. A carpenter by trade, amiable and well respected, he looks down at the sheaf of papers in his hand then turns to his company. "Is everyone here?"

"Best to call them by the characters they play, one by one according to the script," advises the man who guffawed loudly at the actor when his hair caught on fire, a brash but harmless oaf by the name of Bottom, who is a weaver.

Quince takes up one of his papers and looks it over. "Here is a list of those thought fit through all Athens to play in our interlude before the Duke and his Queen, the night of his wedding day."

"First, good Peter Quince," Bottom interrupts, "tell us what the play *deals* with, *then* read the names of the actors, and so make your point."

Quince considers Bottom's suggestion for a moment. "Very well, our play is "The Most Lamentable Comedy, and Most Cruel Death of Pyramus and Thisbe.""

"A very good piece of work, I assure you," Bottom comments authoritatively, "and a merry one too." Assuming Bottom knows what he's talking about, the others nod their heads: Snug, a woodworker still with his tool-belt on and sawdust sprinkled in his hair; Flute, much younger than the rest, a meek and mild tailor; Snout, a seller of pots and pans, samples of his wares dangling from a rope around his waist, the metal clattering as he paces nervously about; and Starveling, a high-spirited chimney-sweep whose face and hands are covered in soot, who easily forgets things.

"Now, good Peter Quince," Bottom continues, "assign the actors to their parts." He waves the men to gather round but when they do they're much too close. "Masters," he scolds, "spread yourselves out."

Quince sees his opportunity and once more reads from his paper. "Answer when I call you. Nick Bottom, the weaver?"

"Ready," he answers. "Tell me what part I have then."

"You, Nick Bottom, are down to play Pyramus."

"What is Pyramus, a lover or a tyrant?"

"A lover who kills himself most gallantly for love."

"That will require some tears in the true performing of it." Arms crossed, he raises a hand to his chin and ponders his role. "If I do it, let the audience beware: I will move them to tears through grief and sorrow! As to the rest—my preference would be to enact the tyrant. I could do Hercules excellently," he wraps Starveling in a crushing bear-hug and hoists him into the air, "a part where I could rant and rave and break everyone up." He lets hapless Starveling go and assumes a dramatic posture. 'The raging rocks, and shivering shocks, shall break the locks, of prison gates!" he roars. "Mighty Apollo across the sky, shining from on high, the weaklings decry, their foolish fates!" The others applaud vigorously, prompting him to a deep bow and a flourish of his hand. "Now *this* is good acting, masters. So," he instructs Quince, "name the rest of the players." But he adds importantly, before Quince can speak, "This is Hercules' style, a tyrant's style: a lover would be more condoning."

Quince frowns at Bottom's use of the wrong word but attempts to carry on.

"Francis Flute the tailor?"

"Here, Peter Quince."

"Flute, you must take on the part of Thisbe."

"What is Thisbe?" he asks, "a wandering knight?"

"She's the lady Pyramus loves."

Flute shakes his head. "Let me not be given the part of a woman—I've got a beard coming in."

"That's neither here nor there," Quince explains, "you shall play it in a wig, and speak with a high-pitched voice." More bad news, Flute puts on a miserable pout and shakes his head in dismay.

"If her head is to be wigged," Bottom swaggers, "let me play Thisbe too. I'll speak in a high squeaking voice—" and he does so, hamming up the part: "'Thisne, Thisne!' 'Oh Pyramus, my lover dear!' 'I am your dear, your Thisbe dear!'"

"No, no," Quince protests, "you must play Pyramus. And Flute, you Thisbe."

"All right, proceed," Bottom says impatiently and takes to gesturing with his hands the way he imagines great actors do, though his flourishes are those of a buffoon.

"Robin Starveling, the chimney-sweep?"

"Here here, Peter Quince."

"Robin Starveling, you must play Thisbe's mother." Starveling nods and accepts his part. "Tom Snout, the merchant of pots and pans?"

"Here, Peter Quince."

"You will be Pyramus's father, myself, Thisbe's father. Snug the woodworker, you will have the lion's part." He lowers his sheet of paper. "And a fitting play I hope our play will be."

"Is the lion's part written?" Snug asks. "If it is, give it me now, for I'm slow with learning."

"You can make it up as you go for it's nothing but roaring."

"Let me play the lion too!" Bottom clamors, "I will roar so that it will do any man's heart good to hear me, and have the Duke clamoring 'Let him roar again—more of this roar!'"

"If you do it too fiercely," cautions Quince, "you'll frighten the Queen and the ladies, and they'll begin screaming: and that would be enough to see us all hanged."

"That would surely hang us," the others mutter and nod.

"I grant you, friends, if we frighten the ladies out of their delicate wits, they would have no choice but to hang us. But I will aggravate my voice so that the roar comes gently as a cooing dove. I will roar as if I were a nightingale—"

"You can't play any part but Pyramus," Quince says, gently reasserting his authority.

Insulted, Bottom turns and storms off, Quince running through the street to catch up to him. "For Pyramus..." Quince scrambles to appease his leading-man, "—he's a good-looking man, a very handsome man, *very* handsome he is." Bottom slows down but is not quite mollified. "A most attractive gentleman is Pyramus, which means only you among us can play the part in our play..."

Bottom stops walking and deliberates. "Well, I will consider it then," he says. "What type of beard would be best to play him in?"

"Any type you choose," Quince concedes and leads him back to rejoin the others.

"I will perform it in either your straw-colored beard," Bottom announces, "your tawny orange beard, your scarlet red, or your burnished beard like they have on gold coins."

"But if the heads on your gold-coins are beardless," frowns Quince, "you'll have to play the part *bare-Bottomed*," he jokes and tweaks the weaver's chin in good fun, though Bottom is not amused. "So, masters," Quince addresses the group, "you have your parts. I entreat you, request you and desire you to learn them by tomorrow night and meet me in the Cerean Wood by moonlight. There we will rehearse, for if we do so here in the city," he scowls and cocks a thumb toward the amphitheater, "we shall be pestered by spectators, and the plot of our play will be known by all beforehand. In the meantime, I will draw up a list of the properties we each will need. I pray you all not to let me down!"

"We will meet, then, and rehearse most obscenely and curvaceously," Bottom says with the utmost conviction. "But remember, friends, get your parts down pat. Adieu, adieu," he bids goodbye, and takes a final dramatic bow that is lost on the other actors: puzzling over the parts they've been given, they amble off along the street. "Be you all there," Bottom warns, "or of Bottom's wrath you'd best beware!"

Shaking his head, Quince turns and goes back to the amphitheater....

Night has fallen deep in the Cerean Wood outside the city of Athens as Puck—the most mischievous of all the gremlin spirits serving Oberon, King of the Fairies—wakes up on his bed of ferns after a long day's sleep beside the waterfall pool, cast now in pale blue light from the moon. Yawning, he slips off the ferns, the fronds promptly springing upright into standing position behind him.

He rubs his eyes and gazes around the forest grove, twitching his small goblin nose, scratching his pointed ears, listening for a moment to the sound the water makes as it courses over the raised rock ledge and spills into the pool below. He goes toward it and kneels down, dipping his cupped hands in the water to splash some on his face. But as he's leaning forward, he notices a small, silver-winged fairy asleep on a nearby lily pad. He chuckles to himself, dips one of his hands again and now flicks water at the fairy who wakes with a start and, frightened, flies off into the moon-blue shadows—just where a spider has woven a wide web between the trunks of two trees. Her wings suddenly caught in the shimmering gossamer strands, the fairy lets out a shriek and calls for help in a tiny petrified voice: a furry-legged black spider is already climbing down the web toward its helpless prey!

Alert to the helpless fairy's plight, Puck hurries around the side of the pool and scoops her up in the palm of his hand, the angry spider jumping at Puck for stealing his dinner: but he's not fast enough for Oberon's wily gremlin and, all six legs frantically clawing the air, the spider misses Puck and plunges toward the waterfall pool, landing, as luck would have it, on one of the floating lily pads where it can do nothing but sit rubbing its front pincers together in ill-tempered disappointment...

"How now, spirit, where are you off to in such a hurry?" Puck asks.

"Over hill, over dale," the fairy pants restlessly in a small but determined voice, "through the bush and through the briar, over park and over pale—through the flood and through the fire. I do wander everywhere," she points to the night sky, "swifter than the moon up there. Sir, I serve the Fairy Queen, I dew the grass upon the green. Flowers tall her night guards be, in their gold coats, spots you'll see: those are rubies, fairy toys, that light the dreams of girls and boys. I must spread my dewdrops now: but gratefully, before you bow." She does so, adding a delicate flourish with her little silver fairy hand. "Farewell, my fellow spirit, I'll be gone: our Queen and all her elves come here anon."

Puck shakes his head uneasily. "The King doth hold his revels here tonight," he warns, "take heed your Queen come not within his sight, for Oberon is mad and waxing wrath because the Queen as her attendant hath a lovely boy, stolen from an Indian king—she never had so sweet an orphan changeling. And jealous Oberon would have the child with him to roam the forests wild: yet she, by force, retains her precious boy, garlands him with flowers, makes of him her pride and joy. So now they never meet in grove or green, by fountain clear or spangled starlight sheen, but quarrel they do in bitterness, and all their elves, for fear, creep quickly under acorn shells and hide there."

The fairy cocks her head, plants a hand on her tiny hip, and gazes up at Puck. "Either I mistake your garb and visage quite, or else you are that shrewd and knavish sprite—the one called Robin Goodfellow. Are not you he that frights the village maidens with such glee, skims the cream from milk they're churning so butter never forms, despite their endless turning? And sometimes keep the farmers' beer from foaming, tricking night wanderers and laughing at their aimless roaming? Those that call you 'Hobgoblin' and 'sweet Puck'—you do their bidding and bring them good fairy luck. Are you not he?"

"You have it rightly," Puck winks and nods, "I am he who wanders nightly, jesting to make King Oberon smile when I the mother horse beguile, neighing like her filly foal—or sometimes hide in the gossip's punch bowl, where changed to the shape of an apple I'll float: on bending to drink, I tickle her throat, and up she jumps with a fearful wail. The old great aunt, mourning over the saddest tale, sometimes for a stool mistakes me—when I slip out from under her bum, tumbling down goes she. 'Devil!' she cries upon the floor and soon falls to coughing—while all the others put hands to their hips and can't stop laughing: in mirth guffawing, they wheeze and swear, a merrier hour was never wasted there," he says, giggling at the recollection—but not for long: a line of moving torches is winding its way through the forest toward them. "Make way, good fairy! Here comes Oberon."

The fairy points to a line of torches approaching from a different direction. "And here my mistress! Would that he were gone!"

Oberon is the first to arrive. A daunting figure clothed in black from head to toe: mask, cape, gloved hands and high boots, he plummets into the moonlit clearing and glides to a stop by the waterfall pool not far from where Puck is standing. His band of fairies and gremlins spreading out then hovering in the air around him, the Fairy King folds his arms and glares coldly at Titania, his Queen, passing in the trees beyond the waterfall clearing with her shining train of sprites and fairy nymphs.

"Ill-met by moonlight, proud Titania!" Oberon thunders.

In an emerald-green mask that matches the green of the glittering gown she's wearing, the Fairy Queen slows her procession down but sees it's Oberon who has called her and tosses him a cold, dismissive sneer. "Still jealous, Oberon?" She flashes her emerald eyes at him for a moment then turns away and motions her fairy band to continue. "Onward fairies, I have renounced his bed and company!"

"No further, wayward woman!" Oberon objects. "Am I not your lord and husband?" And with a wave of his black-gloved hand he dispatches a flight of gremlins to surround the Queen, her nymphs and winged fairies, who cower behind Titania now, frightened of the black-winged goblins.

"Then I must be your wife and lady," she comes back, "—but I know when you steal away from Fairy Land…disguise yourself as a lovelorn shepherd who sits all day and strums his lyre, sadly singing of the shepherdess he loves." Her fairies starting to whimper in fear,

Titania raises her hand and flicks it at the gremlins—*choong!* Rays of green light shoot into their eyes and drive them back to Oberon's side. "Why are you here?" she questions Oberon. "Unless you have come all the way from the coasts of India to meet the bouncing Amazon," she smiles pointedly, "your hunter mistress, your warrior love. Come to wish her and the Duke a long and fruitful marriage? Yes. That must certainly be why you have come."

"How can you even think to question what I do with Hippolyta, knowing that I know about your love for Theseus? Was it not for you that he deserted all the others he wooed and won? Antiope, Ariadne, goddess and mortal alike?"

"These are but the inventions of your too jealous mind. Not once since the start of summer have we met on hill, in dale, or forest, by the waterfall or the rushing brook, the beach along the shore of the sea when the sun is bright—where you know I like to walk and listen to the wind as it whistles in my ears—but you have hounded and provoked me to a fight. This is why the winds, favoring us in vain, it seems, have in revenge now conjured terrible storms and sent them sweeping across the land so even the smallest rivers are bursting at their banks. The oxen strain against their yokes in vain, the ploughman wastes his sweat, and the green corn rots on the stalk unpicked. The sheepfold stands empty in the drowned fields, and scavenger crows are grown fat from feasting on dead wild creatures. The meadow where the country dances are held, is nothing but soggy mud, the tall cedar mazes, the wildflower gardens, are nearly grown invisible from grass too long uncut. The human mortals want their winter cheer: their nights are no longer with hymns or carols blessed. Therefore the moon, ruler of the fog, each night more pale with anger, dampens and mists the airy dark while sleepers take their rest. Contagion spreads and does abound, and due to this intemperate weather the seasons themselves trade their very places: hoary-white frosts freeze the petals on red summer roses, and round old winter's icy head a wreath of fragrant flowers is wound instead. The spring, the summer, bountiful autumn, angry winter—all exchange their natural dress so more and more the bewildered world cannot tell which is which. And these upsetting evils, Fairy King, have come about because of us two quarreling, from our bitterness and dissension: we are the cause, the source of strife."

"Put a stop to it then, there is nothing I can do. Why should Titania so oppose her Oberon? I do but beg an orphan boy to be my page and accompany me."

"Trouble yourself about the boy no more. Your whole fairy kingdom would not buy the child of me. His mother was a devoted friend, and in the spicèd Indian air, by night she often gossiped at my side, and sat with me upon the shore, the two of us watching as merchant ships embarked for distant lands, laughing to see their sails conceive and grow full-bellied from the lusty wind having its blustery way—which she in her dress would imitate, her womb then ripe with my young squire—and would sail around the nearby country to fetch me tokens of her affection, returning again from her own small voyage with marvels rich and pleasing to me. But she, being mortal, succumbed in the labor of giving birth, and very soon after died. It is for her sake that I am raising the boy myself, and for her sake too I will never let him go."

"How long within these woods plan you to stay?"

"Perhaps till after Theseus's wedding day." She peers at him for a moment, her lips curling in a coy smile. "If in our moonlight revels you could calm yourself enough to join, come with us." Oberon shakes his head almost as soon as she stops speaking. "Then let me alone, and your forest haunts my fairies and I will carefully avoid."

"Give me the boy and I will go with thee!" Oberon offers.

"Not for all your fairy kingdom," is her answer. "Fairies, away! The King and I will come to blows if I much longer stay." She takes a fold of her emerald-green gown, swirls it defiantly in Oberon's face then starts her body spinning around, faster and faster so the ferns and trees are bending in the hurricane gust—until suddenly the green spinning light disappears: Titania and her fairy band are gone.

"Go thy way!" Oberon shouts after her, "thou shalt not leave this grove tonight till I repay thee for this trouble!" Fuming in anger, he barks at his gremlins to leave, and a second later they have all dispersed, leaving their disgruntled King alone in the clearing with his faithful helper Puck.

"Come sit," says Oberon, motioning the spirit to join him on the moss-covered rocks along the edge of the waterfall pond.

Puck scurries over and squats down beside the King.

"Gentle Puck, do you remember when once I sat upon the ocean point and heard a mermaid sing the most beautiful song while riding a dolphin's back? That the rough sea grew calm at the sound of her voice, and stars above gathered in the spheres, just to hear the sea-maid's music?"

"I do remember," Puck nods and recalls the occasion.

"That very time I also saw—though you could not—flying between the cold moon and the earth, Cupid with his arrow and bow: most careful with his aim he was, and at a young and pretty maid, enthroned in light from the setting sun, he loosed a love-tipped arrow from his bow, one potent enough to pierce a hundred thousand hearts with love. But I could see young Cupid's shaft by the beams of the rising moon, and in his haste his aim was off, and so the girl passed by in peaceful contemplation, fancy-free. Yet I observed where Cupid's love-bolt fell: it landed in a bank of flowers, milk-white just a moment before love's arrow struck and stained the petals red as blood: pansies, I've heard the maidens call them. Fetch me some of these flowers, these pansies I saw that day. The juice on the sleeping eyelids laid will make both man and woman madly dote upon the next live creature that it sees. Fetch me this herb, and return it here before I have time to wonder why it's taking you so long."

Puck shoots to his feet and bows to the Fairy King. "I'll cover the earth so fast for Oberon, that even *he* won't notice I was gone!" He leaps into the air and flies off...

Oberon gazes into the waterfall pool, where the moon's reflection shimmers between the lily pads, and hatches his plan. "Once I have this juice, I'll steal upon Titania when she's fast asleep and pour its nectar in her eyes. The first thing that she sees upon awaking—be it lion, wolf or bear, meddlesome monkey or angry ape—she shall pursue it in raptures of infatuated love. And ere I lift the spell from off her sight— for I can do so with another herb—I'll make her give the Indian youth to me—" A rustling sound goes up in the forest behind him. "But who comes here?" Oberon wonders and immediately gets to his feet. "I'll make myself invisible and harken to the conversation..." He dashes to the edge of the forest and slips behind a stand of ferns, just as Demetrius enters the clearing, Helena not far behind.

"I love thee not!" Demetrius cries, "therefore pursue me not!" He stops and threatens to draw his sword, which keeps Helena at bay while his eyes search the clearing. "Where are Lysander and fair Hermia? The one I'll slay, the other slayeth me—you told me they had stolen into this wood, yet here am I, and my beloved Hermia I do not see. So get thee gone and no more follow me."

Helena runs at him and flings her arms around his neck. "Cold-hearted though you be, I'm drawn to you as metal to a magnet, and yet my heart, which is true as steel, attracts not you nor makes you feel. If you could lose the power of attraction, I'd lose that power which drives me to distraction."

"Do I encourage you? Do I even speak to you politely? Or do I not in honest truth tell you I *do* not, and always *will* not, love you?"

"In spite of which I love you even more," she pleads and tries to throw her arms around his neck but he pushes her roughly away. "I am your slave, Demetrius, and your hard rebukes only make me crave your love the more. Treat me as you would a spaniel dog, spurn me, strike me, dismiss me and neglect me, only give me leave, unworthy as I am, to follow you in case some day—some hoped for day—you find your feelings change." What lesser place could ever I have within your love—and yet a place that means the world to me—than to be used as you would use your dog, but better that than not to be used at all…"

"You test the limits of my patience—I hate you—it makes me sick to even look upon you."

"And I am sick when I cannot look upon you," she says dejectedly.

"You risk too much by leaving the city as you've done, to press your love on one who loves you not—trusting to the perils of the night and the demon spirits that lurk in such a dark, deserted place. It is dangerous and unwise."

"I care not for myself, Demetrius, and the risk is mine to take. Your goodness is my protection: for it is not night as long as I do behold your face. There is no night at all, nor in these woods do I feel myself alone, for you are the very world to me. How can it be said I am alone, when all the world is here to see?"

"I'll run and hide where you will never find me, and leave you to the mercy of the beasts—"

"The wildest of which has not a heart as cruel as yours! Run where you will, my course will never change: the story holds that Apollo flew from Daphne but she never abandoned her chase. The dove may pursue the griffin, the timid deer may speed and outrun the tiger—but fruitless is speed if cowardice goes after that which valor flees!"

"I'll not endure this reasoning. Let me go, and if you follow me now, don't think I will fear to use thee badly, alone as we are in the wood!"

"As everywhere else you use me badly? For shame, for shame Demetrius! Your wrongs do such discredit to my sex—we cannot fight for love as men may do, since women were not made to woo." Once more she throws her arms around him, struggles to kiss him on the lips. But wrenching himself free, he flings her to the ground and races off into the woods.

Quickly back on her feet, Helena brushes dirt from her clothes. "I'll follow him and make a heaven of hell," she says bravely, "even though I die at the hands of him I love so well." Ever hopeful, she charges into the forest after her Demetrius.

Oberon reappears in the clearing after she is gone. "Fare thee well, nymph. Before he leaves the grove tonight, it shall be he who seeks your love, while you will be the one in flight." He turns to face the waterfall: the soothing the sound of the water as it splashes and froths in the moonlit pool below—when Puck arrives back from his mission.

"Have you the flower there?" he questions anxiously. Puck pouts, hurt that Oberon is not happier to see him. "Welcome, wanderer," says Oberon, and puts a placating arm around his shoulder.

"Yes, my King, I have it here," Puck says and holds up of a handful of red pansy blossoms. Oberon takes several flower sprigs and flashes Puck a gloating smile. "I know a bank where the wild thyme blows, where honeysuckle and purple violets grow, overhung with luscious vines, with musk-scented roses and dove-white columbines. There Titania sleeps most nights, lolling on this bed of flowers, while fairies dance and sing for her delight—where the snakes cast off their skin, garments for fairies to wrap themselves in. And with the juice of this

I'll streak her eyes, to make her full of hideous fantasies. Take you some of it too, and find within this forest grove a sweet Athenian lady who's in love but with a cold and scornful youth. Anoint his sleeping eyes and do it so the next thing that he spies may be that lady. You will know the man by the Athenian garments he has on. Do it with especial care, that he may prove more doting fond of her, than ever she felt pangs of love for him. And then be sure you meet me ere the morning rooster crows."

"Fear not, my Lord, your humble servant goes!" Up and away, Puck soars into the night, his beating wings in dark silhouette as he passes in front of the bright shining moon, which has never looked so full, so round, so white....

Titania reclines on the flowered bank where the stream bends gently in another part of the forest, her band of winged fairies and elfin spirits working to prepare their weary Queen for bed: some are brushing her long auburn hair, some spreading the folds of her emerald gown on the ground around her feet, some fly up behind her head and start removing her emerald-green mask—but Titania stops them with a shake of her head and sweeps her hand through the air.

"Come, fairies, and dance for me, and sing your fairy song! Then off to the sky I order you all to be gone: some to save the May-time buds from greedy, munching pests, some to hunt the long-eared bats for leathery wings from which to make my small elves coats. And some keep quiet the noisy owl that nightly hoots and wonders at our fairy fest. Sing me now asleep, then to your duties each, and let me rest."

A fairy takes to the air and hovers in front of the Queen. "*Beware you, spotted snakes with poison tongues,*" she sings in a dream-soft voice, "*sharp-quill hedgehogs be not seen! Newts and lizards, do no wrong—come not near our Fairy Queen.*"

"*O nightingale, your melody,*" the elves and fairies chorus in, "*sing in our sweet lullaby: lulla, lulla, lullaby. Never charm, nor spells, nor harm, come our lovely lady nigh—only this our lullaby.*"

The first fairy continues. *"Weaving spiders, come not here. Hence you long-legged insects, hence! Beetles black, approach not near, nor worms, nor snails commit offence!"*

"O nightingale your melody, sing in our sweet lullaby..." The others take up the chorus briefly, but a second fairy sees Titania has drifted off to sleep and waves the the elves and fairies to be silent. "Hence we go, away!" she whispers. "All is well. But some remain as sentinels." She appoints a dozen fairies to stay behind and guard the Queen while the others assemble in silver-winged platoons and, on a signal from the second fairy, sail off in all directions to do the bidding of their Queen. The fairy guards descend and light on the canopy of vines under which Titania lies sleeping. Yawning as they take up their positions, it isn't long before their eyes are closed and they are slumbering too, the forest perfectly quiet and still, the moonlight a ghostly blue...

But Oberon has been lurking in the trees not far away. He swiftly glides from his hiding place and kneels beside Titania. "What you see when you awaken, let it for your love be taken. Love and languish as one forsaken. Be it lynx, or cat, or bear, leopard or boar with bristled hair, to your eyes it shall appear, as that most precious, that most dear. Wake when some vile thing is near!" He leans down and squeezes the pansy flowers so Cupid's nectar drips on her eyes. One of the fairies stirs in her sleep. Her eyes blink open and she peers below...but all is as it should be: Oberon has done his work and gone...

*

Lysander and Hermia wander from the woods and stop at the edge of the waterfall clearing. Their clothes and possessions in bundles on their backs, they look worried and exhausted, especially Hermia, who stumbles while crossing the clearing but Lysander is there to catch her:

"Fair love, you are faint from wandering in the wood, and the fault is all mine for losing the way." He looks around. "We'll rest here if you think it good, then carry on by light of day."

"Be it so," she says and puts her bundle down. Gazing at the waterfall, she kneels on the ground and taking her bundle, places it at the foot of a tree. "You should find yourself a bed, for here is where I'll lay my head."

Lysander comes over and kneels down, taking her hands in his. "One piece of ground our pillow green—one heart, one bed, one love between." He kisses her.

"For your love's sake, my dear, lie further off, be not so near."

"That's *not* what my words meant," he says. "My thoughts, I promise, were innocent. I only mean my heart to yours is knit: a single heart—from two—we've made of it. Two bosoms intertwined with love's firm oath—two bosoms but a single truth for both. Come," he says and takes her hands again, "by your side no bed-room me deny, for lying apart from Hermia I do not lie."

"Lysander riddles cleverly," she says and pulls away. "You're right to curse my caution and my pride, if Hermia meant to say Lysander lied!" She stands up. "But, gentle friend, out of love and courtesy lie further off, respecting women's modesty. Such separation seems more fitting for a virtuous bachelor and his maid, so keep your distance here," she points to a spot on the ground near the waterfall pool, "and good night, sweet friend: I pray your love will never change till your sweet life is at its end."

"Amen to that fair prayer, say I. And end my life if ever I break my vow to thee." He tries to kiss her but she takes a step back. "Here is my bed," he smiles. "Sleep give you blissful rest."

"With half that wish the wisher's sleep be blessed," she says, steps forward and kisses him on the cheek. He starts to speak but she silences him with a finger to his lips.

She returns to her bed and lies down, listening with her eyes open to the steady sound of the waterfall nearby. In a moment she gets drowsy, her eyes close, and soon she drifts off to sleep...

"Through the forest have I gone, but Athenian found I none, upon whose eyes this flower's juice the force of love I might let loose." Sprigs of the red magic flower in his hand, Puck marches out of the woods. "Night and silence," he says and sighs. "Night and silence..." He sighs again and shakes his head, dismayed. "But who is there?" He spots Lysander and hastens over. He rejoices: "Athenian garments he does wear: this is he my master said despised the poor Athenian maid!"

He turns and looks about, noticing Hermia asleep by the trees. He flits over and gazes down at her. "And here the maiden sleeping sound, on the dank and dirty ground. Pretty soul, she dares not lie near this unloving brute that only makes her cry." Back to Lysander, he kneels down and holds out the red magic flower. "Cruel heart, upon your eyes I throw, the magic power this nectar does bestow." He puts the juice on Lysander's eyes. "When you waken, your love will be, for this young woman who so loves thee! And so awake when I am gone, for I must now to Oberon." He leaps into the air and soars off above the trees. The lovers sleeping soundly, all goes back to night and silence again...

"—I know you want to kill me, sweet Demetrius," Helena's voice rings out in the forest.

"—I told you, stay away!" snaps Demetrius, "I forbade you to stalk me thus!" Crashing through a thicket of bushes, he bursts into the clearing with Helena charging forward behind him.

"Don't leave me alone in the dark, " she pleads, "do not so!"

"Fend for yourself—" Demetrius pants "—on my own through the forest I'll go!" He streaks across the clearing, ducks back into the woods, then away.

Although she could still go on, Helena pulls up at the waterfall pool, unhappy and dismayed. "I am out of breath from this lovesick chase. It seems the harder that I try, the more I am disgraced," she says and almost starts to cry. "Lucky Hermia, wherever she lies, for she has beautiful and brilliant eyes." Sighing, she sits on some rocks beside the pool. "—How came her eyes to be so bright?" she broods. "Surely not with sad tears. If so, mine are more often washed than hers. No, no I am even more ugly than a bear, for beasts that meet me run away in fear. Little wonder that Demetrius, as he would from a very monster, flies from my presence thus. What wretched and deceiving mirror of mine, made me think my dullness could compete with Hermia's shine? But who is there...?" She stands up and takes a closer look. "Lysander, on the ground? Dead or asleep? I see no blood, no wound." Confused, she kneels down and shakes him by the shoulders. "Lysander, if you live, good sir, awake!"

He sits up, transfixed by her face. "And run through fire I will for thy sweet sake! Radiant, Helena," he clutches her by the arms,

"Nature's magic art has opened my eyes to your tender heart!" He glances behind her. "But where is Demetrius? O how fit a word is that vile name to perish on my sword!"

She gets to her feet and steps back from him. "Do not say so, Lysander, say not so! He loves only Hermia—and Hermia loves only you, so be content."

"Content with Hermia? No, I do repent the tedious minutes with her I've ever spent. It's Hermia no longer, but Helen who I love! Who would not exchange a raven for a dove? Our human will by reason is swayed, and reason tells me *you* are the worthier maid. Things that grow are not ripe until their season: so I, being young, can only now see reason—till now had not the lover's skill to let my reason guide my will—it leads me to your eyes," he kneels at her feet, "and in them, when I look, I see the story of our love, written in love's richest book."

"Why was I to such mean mockery born? Why, at your hands, do I deserve such scorn? Is it not enough," Helena demands, "is it not enough, cruel man, that I did never—no, nor ever can—win one sweet look from Demetrius's eye, but you must mock me with love's impassioned cry? In truth, you do me wrong, in such disdainful manner me to woo." She backs toward the trees. "But fare you well—indeed I must confess, I thought you a man of more true gentleness. O that a lady, by one man refused, should by another find herself abused!" Hurt and ashamed, she turns away from him and flees.

He jumps to his feet and glances across the clearing. "She sees not Hermia," he says to himself. "Hermia, stay sleeping here. And nevermore Lysander come near! For as excess of the sweetest things the worst discomfort to the stomach brings, or as the lies men stop believing, are hated most by those they've been deceiving, so you, my excess—my lie—by all be hated, but most of all by me. All my powers, my strength and might, bend yourselves to honor Helen, to be her love, her knight!" He rushes to gather his belongings together, bundles them up, and without so much as a glance at Hermia he charges into the forest after Helena.

Hermia slumbers on in the moonlight, stirring slightly with a dream she is having. She mumbles in her sleep—babbled words that make no sense—then suddenly her arms are thrashing and she's crying in the throes of violent nightmare: "Help me, Lysander, help me!" she screams. "Pluck this crawling serpent from my breast!" She awakes and sits up, panting breathlessly while slowly the bad dream subsides. "What a fright," she says shivering, "what a dream was here! Lysander, look how I shake with fear!" She rises and walks past the waterfall pool. "A sickening serpent was eating my heart away and you sat smiling as I became his prey—" She halts in alarm. "Lysander, departed? Lysander, my lord!" she calls. "Lysander!" She turns and makes sure he is really gone, that she's not still dreaming. "Gone? No sound? Not a word? Pray, Lysander, where *are* you? Speak, if you can hear, for love's sake! I tremble in desperate fear!" She listens for the sound of his voice. "Nothing?—Then it must be you are gone away. Give me death, or let me find you without delay!" She runs back and quickly bundles her things, but unlike the others, Hermia is wary of leaving the moonlit clearing. After several deep breaths and a last look round, she ventures toward the darkness, alone....

Cursing whoever's idea it was to travel to the forest, Bottom untangles his arms and legs from a bramble bush that won't let go, and stumbles into the moonlit clearing, not far from where Titania and her fairy guards are sound asleep in their bed of vines and flowers.

"Where's the others?" he wonders out loud.

"They're coming," says Quince, next to arrive in the clearing. He looks around and smiles. "This is the perfect place for our rehearsal!" He points to one area. "This green spot will do for a stage, this hawthorn thicket," he points behind the bushes, "our changing area can be. We'll do the play just as we will for the Duke," he says, eager and most enthused.

"Peter Quince," Bottom says, taking out his crumpled copy of the script.

"What is it, my good Bottom?"

"There are things in this comedy of Pyramus and Thisbe which people are sure not to like. Take the part wherein Pyramus must draw a sword to kill him self. The ladies will be horror-fried by such a frightening act. What do you say to that?"

"A worthy fear, good Bottom," Snout pipes up and enters the clearing with Starveling, who as Thisbe's mother is all decked out in a gaudy dress and a poorly made long-haired wig. Pillows and cushions are stuffed in the dress to make him look fat and…large-breasted.

Unnoticed by the others, Flute and Snug emerge from the woods and saunter into the clearing, both a little tipsy from the bottle of ale they've been sharing.

"I say we leave the killing out, when all is said and done," Starveling suggests to Quince, who, with a hand over his mouth, chortles at Starveling's outlandish costume.

"—Not at all," Bottom disagrees. "For I have the perfect change to our plot: write me a prologue to speak beforehand, and let this prologue seem to say no harm will be done with the swords we draw, and that Pyramus is not killed in the end, after all. And for more assurance than this, I'd say, this prologue should tell them that I, Pyramus, am not Pyramus either, after all, but only Bottom the weaver. *That* will keep the ladies from being pro-turbed."

"Well," says Quince, considering the suggestion, "we *could* have such a prologue. We'll have it written in iambic pen-*ta*meter, five beats to the line."

"No, make it seven, an even seven," Bottom suggests instead.

Snout looks at Starveling who counts his fingers, more than a little confused. "But won't the ladies be more afraid of the lion?"

Starveling gives up on his fingers and brushes back a strand of longer hair that has fallen across his face. "I can tell you, that's what *I'd* be afraid of."

The others look at him, surprised.

"Afraid of the lion?" asks Snout.

"No, the *ladies*," Starveling clarifies. "I fear it, I can tell you." He adjusts the two pillows that are serving as his bosoms.

"Masters," Bottom says, siding with Starveling, "ask yourselves this: is it not a most dreadful thing to put a lion before the ladies? Why, there's no more fearful wild-fowl on earth than a mighty roaring lion."

"Wild-fowl?" Quince frowns.

"We ought to look into it," Bottom nods, pondering a page of his script.

Snout reflects on the matter. "Mustn't there be a second prologue, then, which tells them he is not a lion?"

"No," says Bottom, "you call him by his name." He explains: "His face will be seen through the lion's mane. And speaking in his usual voice, creates the same defect, like so: 'Ladies,'" he pronounces, "or, 'Fair ladies, I beg you,' or 'I would request you,' or 'I would beseech you, not to be afraid, not to shake and tremble, on my life! If you think I am a lion, would my life not be in danger? No, I am *not* in danger, for I am just a man, like any other.' So by all means let him use his own name, and tell them plainly he is Snug, the woodworker, after all."

"Fine," Quince acquiesces, "that is how it shall be. But there's still two troubling things to me: one being how the moonlight shall be brought inside the chamber at the Duke's, for as you know, Pyramus and Thisbe meet by moonlight."

"Will the moon be shining the night we do our play?" Snout inquires.

"A calendar! A calendar!" Bottom calls out in alarm. "Look in the almanac, check the moon, check on the moon!"

"Yes, the moon will shining that night," Quince reassures him.

"Why then," Bottom asserts, "you can build a window to put on our stage and leave it open so the moon can shine in."

"Yes, or else someone can appear with a branch and a lantern, and say he is playing Moonlight. Plus, there is one more thing to consider: we need a wall between Pyramus and Thisbe, for the story has it they talked to each other through a hole within a wall."

"You can't use a wall—a standing wall?" asks Snout in disbelief. "What do you say of the wall, Bottom?"

"Someone will have to play the wall," he concedes. "Have plaster upon him, or clay or mortar, which will show that he's playing a wall. And let him hold his fingers like this," he touches his thumb and finger together and holds them to form a circle. "Pyramus and Thisbe may whisper through the cranny to each other, or even perchance, place a hole where it's needed."

"If that can work, then we are ready," announces Quince, anxious to begin. "Come then, gather round. Arrange yourselves in place, good masters, and let our rehearsal commence." He turns to Bottom. "Pyramus, you will start. When you've said your lines, step back behind the bushes yonder. And the same will hold for the rest of you, once I've given the cue."

But getting the acting underway is easier said than done. Bottom is unhappy with the spot where Quince has placed him, and shifts his ground while Quince attempts to stop the fight that Flute and Snug are having over the last of their bottle of ale. And Snout, for fun, has spread out his arms so Starveling can try to knock him down with his great, billowing bosoms.

Looking on from the forest where he leans against a tree, Puck lets out a chuckle. "What bungling bumpkins have we here, so near the bed of the Fairy Queen? What, a play underway? I'll listen in but keep my distance, act a part if given the chance…" He comes closer but stays out of sight.

His patience exhausted, Quince throws up his hands and retreats to a place near the trees. "Speak, Pyramus!" he shouts at Bottom. "Thisbe," he orders Flute, "step forward."

"*Thisbe, the flowers of odious fragrance sweet—*" says Bottom.

"Odorous," Quince corrects him. "Odorous."

"*—odorous fragrance sweet,*" Bottom continues, "*as is your breath, my dearest Thisbe dear.*" Bottom makes a face, having caught a whiff of the beer on Flute's breath.

Quince points to Snug, standing at the edge of the clearing awaiting his cue. He nods to Quince, cups his hands around his mouth and calls, "A voice! A voice!"

"*But hark!*" Bottom says, and cups a hand behind his ear. "*A voice! Stay but here a little while,*" he says to Flute as Thisbe, "*and soon enough I'll reappear.*" Quince motions to him and he heads behind the bushes over to one side.

"A stranger Pyramus than ever played around here," Puck quips and ducks back into the forest.

"Must I speak now?" asks Flute.

"Yes, you must," Quince urges, "for you know Pyramus goes—"

"Pyramus?"

"Bottom!" Quince barks. "—He goes but to see the cause of the noise, and then he returns again."

Flute nods, understanding. "*Most radiant Pyramus, most lily-white in* hue," he recites with emphasis on the final syllable, but he's speaking so slowly that Quince rolls his finger, motioning him to speed up. "*Of color like the red rose on glorious briars, most briskly youth-full and delicate as morning dew,*" he says all at once then gasps as he takes a breath, "*as faith-full as the faith-fullest horse that never tires—I'll meet thee, Pyramus, at Ninny's tomb."*

"*Ninus's* tomb," Quince corrects him. "But you don't say that just yet. That's what you say to Pyramus."

"Pyramus?"

"Bottom," Quince reminds him again. "You say only the first part. Pyramus, enter!" he calls, "you missed your cue. 'Never tires.'"

"O," Flute repeats the line, "as faith-full—"

"Faithful," Quince helps.

"—As faithful as the faithfulest horse that never yet has—" But he stops. His jaw draws open: Puck has sent Bottom into the clearing but he's been transformed into a donkey from the shoulders up. He has the head, ears and snout of a live ass.

"*If I were handsome, Thisbe*," he exclaims, "*I would only be yours alone!*"

"O ghastly sight!" shrieks Quince. "O hideous—the woods are haunted! Fly, masters, fly!" He makes for the trees and the others are right behind him, frightened and running fast.

"I'll follow you," Puck snickers, "I'll lead you round and round! Through bog, through bush, through prickly bramble briar—a horse I'll be, perhaps a hound, a hog, a headless bear, perhaps a ball of fire. I'll neigh and bark, I'll squeal and growl and burn—like fire at every turn!" He speeds after the fleeing actors…

Bottom yells after them but his voice becomes the hee-haw bray of a donkey. "Why do they run away?" he wonders in his own voice. "This must be some trick of theirs to scare me out of my wits!"

Snout having got separated from the others, calls out from the edge of the clearing: "Bottom, you're changed! What do I see has happened to thee?"

"What do you see? You see your assinine self, that's what!" Bottom gripes, annoyed. He walks toward Snout, but he's not going to wait for an answer to his question, and he runs off.

Quince pokes his head out from behind some bushes and calls out in pity. "Bless you, Bottom, bless you! How terrible a transformation!" But when Bottom bounds toward him, he tears away in the forest.

"I see what you're doing!" Bottom hollers, but again his voice becomes a donkey's bray. "They're out to make an ass of me, to scare me if they can. But I will not budge an inch, no sir, despite the pranks they play. I will just meander here and let them hear my boistering song, and they'll know I'm not afraid. 'The blackbird sings at the dead of night, a tune both sad and sweet," he sings, "'the woodland thrush its voice so bright, joins in as does the wren, tweet-tweet!'"

Over on her bed of flowers, Titania begins to awaken. "What angel serenades me in my flowery bed?"

"'The finch, the sparrow, and the lark, the cuckoo bird in spring, whose taunt is heard by many a man, when his love another is wooing. Yet who but an ass, would heed the to-doing, of a bird that spends its life cuckooing! Not me! Not Bottom, that's who!"

Entranced by the sound of his singing, Titania has arisen and come over to stand before Nick Bottom. She gazes into his eyes. "I pray thee, gentle mortal, sing again. Mine ear is much enamored with thy voice, mine eye enthralled with thy appearance, and thy fair virtue's excellence doth force me at first sight to say, to swear, I love thee!"

"Methinks, madam," he replies, "there's little reason for that. And yet, in truth, reason and love are not the best of friends these days. More's the pity that even some who were good friends, will not come back and make amends." Titania is running her hands over his chest and shoulders. "But I can joke with the best of them on occasion," he declares, oblivious, it seems, to Titania's passionate advances.

"Thou art as wise as thou art handsome," she swoons, and embraces him.

"On that I would disagree with thee, but if I had the wisdom to get out of this wood, that's wisdom enough for me."

She rests her head against his chest. "Out of this wood thou must not go, thou must remain here, if thou wantest to or no! I am a spirit from a higher sphere, the seasons to my will adhere, and I tell you, dear, love thee—therefore say you'll stay with me." She puts her arms around him, her eyes searching his face. "I'll give thee servant fairies to be at your beck and call, they'll tend you and obey you without fail, they'll fetch you treasures from the deep, and sing while thou on fragrant flowers sleep. I'll purge thee of thy mortal grossness so—thou shalt like an airy spirit go!" She pulls away from Bottom, and waves her hand in the air. "Peaseblossom! Cobweb! Mustardseed and Moth!"

From a cloud of glistening gold dust that she causes to appear, elfin creatures spring to life: four little men with features and faces in every way the same. In cutaway suits of various colors, they snap to attention and rush to obey their Queen.

"Ready!" says Peaseblossom, his suit of apple green.

"And I!" from Cobweb, his suit rich cinnamon brown.

"And I!" Moth answers, his jacket and britches of iris blue.

"And I!" declares Mustardseed, in a coat and pants of deepest yellow.

"Where shall we go?" they ask in unison.

"Be kind and courteous to this gentle man. Skip before him, dance in his sight, his tender eyes fill up with delight. Feast him full with apricots and cherries, with figs and grapes and sweet mulberries. Honeycombs steal from the bumble-bees, and with their wax make candles arise, light them using fire-flies, to lead my love away to bed, and by your Queen lay down his head. Pluck the wings from butter-flies, to shade the moonbeams from his eyes—bow to him, elves, and show him all your courtesies."

"Hail, mortal!"

"Hail!"

"Hail!"

"Hail!"

Two to each side, they gather round Bottom and prepare to escort him away. But he resists when they lead him off.

"I heartily beg your worships' pardon.—I beseech you," he says and looks to the elf in cinnamon brown. "Your worship's name?"

"Cobweb."

Bottom reaches down and shakes his hand. "Most happy to make your acquaintance, Cobweb. I look forward to knowing you better." He looks to one of the others. "Your name, good sir?"

"Peaseblossom."

Again he reaches down to shake hands. "I look forward to knowing you better, sir.—And your name?" he glances at the third little man.

"Mustardseed."

"Of course," chuckles Bottom and smiles at the yellow livery the man is wearing.

"It will be a pleasure to know you better, sir." He turns to address the last little man, but Titania has grown impatient. Clouds of mist are billowing out of the forest now and swirling in the clearing.

"Come, my elves, and lead us away. This is no place for lovers to stay: methinks the dew begins to fall—" Bottom lets out a loud, honking bray as he and Titania are swept away and swallowed up in clouds of mist. "—But tell me, love," the Queen inquires, "did I just hear a donkey call?"

Oberon is biding his time by the waterfall pool, watching as his goblins play a game with the fish, though the fish are winning: swimming between the legs of the spirits who splash through the water trying to catch them—swimming in ever widening circles till the flustered goblins grow dizzy and sit down, cursing their luck but vowing they'll get even the next time.

Snickering to himself, Oberon turns away and gazes up at the moon. "I wonder if she's wakened yet…and what she laid her eyes on first—which she will love with quenchless thirst." His lips curl into a gloating smile. "But here comes my messenger. How now, mad spirit?" he calls to Puck, "what is there to tell? What nighttime mischief are up to, here within the forest dell?"

Puck lights on the ground and hurries over to the King, bursting to deliver his news. "Your mistress with an animal is in love!" Oberon shakes his head *No!* Puck nods his head *Yes!* "Close to her secluded bower," he relays the story, "upon her bed of wildflowers, where she'd been sleeping for several hours, oafish, bungling menials, who ply their trades in the market stalls, were gathered together to practice a play, intended for Theseus's wedding day. The dimmest blockhead in their cast, who Pyramus played with brute bombast, went off their stage and entered the trees," he winks at Oberon, "—I took advantage as I pleased: an ass's head I fixed on his noggin. Anon, and Thisbe calls upon him, then forth the foolish actor comes, one look is enough—the others are stunned, and into the forest, running go!" He folds his arms across his chest, " a piece of goblin cunning, no?"

Oberon nods and motions him to go on with the story: Puck continues. "With their senses thus astounded, they stumbled through the forest, confounded, and as they made their way along, cursed the ghosts that were doing them wrong—nettles and thorns at their garments snatching, on sleeves, on pants, on their crude clothes catching, I led them further, confused and scared, and left sweet Pyramus the donkey there—when just that moment it came to pass, Titania waked, and straightway loved an ass!"

Oberon flashes another gloating smile—"This is better than ever I devised. But did you juice the Athenian's eyes as I did bid thee do?"

Puck nods. "Of course—when he was sleeping—that is finished too—and the Athenian woman by his side—so when she waked, he'd be the first she spied."

Shooting a glance across the clearing, Oberon suddenly motions for quiet: Hermia thrashes her way through the trees and dashes out of the woods, Demetrius pursuing fast right behind her.

"Stand back," whispers Oberon, "this is the young Athenian!"

"This is the woman," Puck frowns, "but this is not the man…"

They retreat to a vantage point behind the ferns and look on as Demetrius, not watching where he's going, trips over a mossy log and falls. Hermia keeps her distance from him, out of breath and panting.

"O why refuse you him that loves you so?" he demands and rubs his twisted ankle. "Your words so bitter—as if I were a hated foe!"

"This is but scolding, I could treat you much worse, for you, I fear, have given me cause to curse. If you have slain Lysander in his sleep—spilled his blood already—plunge your knife in deep, and kill me too. The sun was not so loyal to the day, as Lysander was to me! Would he have left his sleeping Hermia? I'd believe that the earth could be struck by the moon, and it bore a hole to the bottom of the sea—and right the way through to th'Antipodes—before I'd believe Lysander—my love—would steal away from me." She crouches down and clutches his tunic. "It can only be that you have murdered him—this is how a murderer looks, so dead, so grim."

"No, this is how the murdered look—that's what you have done to me! Your love has hurt me fatally, yet you, the murderer, look bright and dear, as glimmering Venus in her star-lit sphere."

"What's this to my Lysander?" she exclaims. "Where is he?" She shakes him. "O good Demetrius, will you give him back to me?"

"I'd rather feed his carcass to the hounds."

"Out, dog!" She pummels him with her fists. "Out cur!" He hides behind his upraised arms. "You've driven me past the bounds of honest patience! Have you killed him then? Henceforth be never counted among men. Once and for all, tell me the truth—the truth, Demetrius, for my poor heart's sake, dared you to look upon him, being awake, and have you killed him sleeping?" Demetrius can only gaze longingly into her eyes. "O fatal touch!" she cries, and gets to her feet. "Would not a snake, a stinging adder, harm him just as much? An adder did it," she tells herself and turns to face Demetrius "for with a more vile and poisoned tongue—you serpent, you—never has an adder stung!"

"You waste your feelings on a mistaken guess. I am not guilty of Lysander's death, nor is he dead, at least as far as I can tell."

Her hopes renewed, she crouches down again. "I pray you tell me then that he is well!"

He plays coy. "And if I could, what would I get from Hermia therefore?"

"The privilege of never seeing me more," she answers strangely, and rises quickly to her feet. "And from your hated presence thus I go—see me no more, whether he be dead, or no!" He reaches out to stop her, but she has no trouble eluding him and races into the dark night woods, leaving him alone and brooding.

"Following her now would only be in vain, here therefore a while I shall remain." He heaves a weary sigh. "So sorrow's pain doth heavier grow—a debt to bankrupt sleep my sorrow owes—which now in some small measure I will pay, by resting here until the break of day." He lies down and soon drifts off to sleep.

Oberon and Puck come out of hiding.

"What have you done?" the King demands, enraged. "You didn't get it right—you've laid the magic potion on her true love's sight! From your mistake, thanks to you, a true love's ruined, and not a false turned true."

"Then Fate has intervened against us both—a million fail, but I am one who always keeps his oath," vows Puck.

"About the wood go swifter than the wind, and Helena of Athens try to find. All love-sick she is, and weeping drearily, with sighs of love that pain her dearly. Through some magic bring her here—I'll charm his eyes for when she appears."

"I go, I go, look how fast I go!" He jumps into the air, his wings beginning to beat with a fury, "—I go, I go, swifter than an arrow from Hercules' bow!" Up and away, he soars off into the night, a sparkling comet tail of light disappearing behind him…

Oberon, meanwhile, has crept up on the sleeping Demetrius and, taking the nectar of Cupid's flower, squeezes drops of potion in his eyes. "Flower of this heart-red hue, hit with Cupid's arrow true, be the apple of his eye, when his love he doth espy—let her shine more bright than Venus, nightly in the starry sky!" He looks down at Demetrius. "When thou wakest, if she be here, beg her to be your lover dear!" He slips the magic flower under his cape and gets to his feet, pleased to see, a short moment later, that Puck has returned from his recent flight.

"Captain of our fairy band, Helena is here at hand, and the youth mistook by me, pleading for love's remedy. Shall we their sad spectacle see? Lord, what fools these mortals be!"

"Stand aside. The noise they make will cause Demetrius to wake."

"Then will two at once woo one—that will be outlandish fun." He claps his hands, giddy with delight. "I always find those things which please me, are those that end up preposterously."

Once more they move out of view among the ferns at the edge of the clearing, just at the moment when Helena rushes forward, stops running and sighs, as tired now as she is dejected.

"How could you think that I would woo in scorn?" Lysander pleads upon arriving. "Scorn and contempt don't show themselves through tears—every vow I make to you, is cause to make me weep, and vows, thus born, in the manner of their making truth appears. How can these things in me seem scornful to you, when my tears are a badge of faith that proves them true?"

"You show your cunning more and more! When truth kills truth, twice as deadly is the fray! These vows to me are Hermia's—is your love for her now over? Weigh oath with oath, and there's nothing to weigh: your vows to her and me, put on two scales, will weigh the same and both as light as gossip tales."

"I showed no judgment when to her my love I swore!"

"And just as little, it seems to me, when here you swear you'll never love her more!"

"Demetrius loves her, he loves not you!"

Awakened by their voices, Demetrius sits up, his eyes transfixed in blinding love.

"O Helen, goddess, nymph divine! To what, my love, shall I compare these eyes of thine? Crystal never had so bright a shine!" He gets to his feet and, limping slightly, runs to embrace her. "How ripe the red in your lips doth show—those kissing cherries more tempting grow!" He tries kissing her but she shoves him away. "O let me have your kiss," he pleads, "princess of pure and perfect bliss!" He moves to embrace her again, but Lysander runs and tackles him and their fists begin to fly.

"O spite!" shrieks Helena, "O hell to see the both of you so bent, on teasing me but for your merriment! If you were civil, knew even a little courtesy, you wouldn't do me this injury! Cannot you hate me— I know you do—without joining forces to mock me too?" The fighting is fast and furious on the ground, but there's nothing Helena can do to make them stop. "—If you were men, as in the world you go, you'd not abuse a gentle lady so: to vow, and swear and praise my parts, when I am sure you hate me in your hearts." She tries to make them listen. "—You both are rivals, in love with Hermia, yet now you rival in mocking Helena! A fine display," she shouts with sarcasm, "how manly such an enterprise—to conjure tears in a poor maid's eyes! No man of valor—of noble sort—would offend a woman and thus extort, her poor soul's patience, all to make your sport!"

"You are cruel, Demetrius," Lysander yells, pinning his arms to the ground. "Be not so, for you love Hermia—this you *know* I know: and here, with all good will—with all my heart—to you my love for Hermia I give in every part, and yours, for Helena, to me bequeath, for her I love and will unto my death."

"Never did mockers waste more idle breath!" scoffs Helena.

"Lysander, keep your Hermia!" Demetrius cries and throws Lysander off, "I will have her not. If ever I did love her, that love is now forgot. My heart with her, but as a guest sojourned—and now, to Helen, it has to home returned, there forever to remain."

"Helen, it is not so!" Lysander exclaims.

"Question not the love you do not know," Demetrius comes back, "or face the peril of punishment severe. Look, there your love comes—yonder is thy dear!"

Hermia has come into the waterfall clearing but approaches the others warily.

"Dark night that from the eyes their seeing takes, the ear more quick at apprehending makes, diminishing the seeing sense, it gives to hearing twice the strength. Not with eyes, Lysander, were you found, but my ears, I can be thankful, drew me to your sound. Why didst thou unkindly leave me so?"

"Tell me why a man should stay, when love is pressing him to go," he says, sullen and resentful.

"What love could press Lysander, to suddenly leave my side?"

"Lysander's love, that would not with you let him bide, and fair Helena, who more illumines darkest night than all yon glittering orbs of light. Why do you seek me? Surely this will make you know the hate I bear thee made me love you so?"

"You speak not from the heart—it cannot be!"

"Why, she is of the conspiracy" cries Helena, distraught. "Now I see, you've come together all three, to have your fun and games in spite of me." She glares at them. "Vicious Hermia, you enemy friend, are you with them in their intent to treat me with such cruel contempt? Are all the secrets we have shared, the sisters' vows we pledged, the hours that were so happily spent—is all forgot? *We*, Hermia, two kindred spirits, have sat and stitched the same embroidered flower, together on one cushion, both humming one song in the same melodious key—as if our hands, our sides, our voices and very minds were united in one body. So we grew up in friendship together, like double cherries—separate seeming—and yet, as I say, forever together, two lovely berries joined at the stem—two different bodies, but only one heart—will now you split this love apart, to join with such despicable men, in scorning your oldest and dearest friend?"

"I stand bewildered," says Hermia, "I scorn you not. It seems instead that *you* scorn *me*."

"Have you not set Lysander, in mockery to follow me?" Helena persists. "—To worship my eyes and praise my face—and made this other, Demetrius—who not but several minutes ago, disparaged and discarded me—was it not he you set to calling me goddess, nymph, divine and rare, most precious and beyond compare? Why speaks he thus to her he hates? And why does Lysander deny what is so rich within his soul, and offer me, in seeming truth, his heart's affections whole, but that you, Hermia, set him to it—nay, gave him your consent!" She sadly drops her chin. "Even though I be not so in favor as you are—so hung upon with love, most miserable I am because I love, yet am not loved which you should pity, Hermia, rather than despise."

"I understand not *what* you mean by this," Hermia replies, offended.

"O, but I think you do," Helena comes back. "I'm not so blind but I can't see pretended looks of sadness, the faces that you make behind my back—the way you wink and jest with one another. If you had any pity, grace or manners, you would not make of me the butt of this your joke. But fare ye well, 'tis partly my own fault…which death or disappearance soon shall remedy."

"Stay, gentle Helena," Lysander gets down on his knees, takes her hands, "hear the reasons why you are my love, my life, my soul—my fairest Helena!"

"O excellent!" she cries, sarcastic.

"My sweet, do not scorn her so," Hermia begs Lysander.

"If she cannot persuade you," Demetrius warns Lysander, "I, with all that's in me, will compel you to relent."

Lysander gets to his feet. "You cannot compel me any more than she can persuade—your threats have no more strength than her weak prayers." He turns. "Helen, I love thee, on my life I do, and swear I am wholly willing, to lose it now for you, to prove but false the man who says Lysander loves thee not."

"I know that I love you more than he could ever do," Demetrius glares at Lysander.

"Prepare to fight and prove it true."

"Ready I am for you!"

They lock arms and grapple fiercely, Hermia working to pull Lysander free. "What can be the point of this?" she cries and clutches him around the neck.

"Away, shrew!" but she holds him tight, Demetrius standing back.

"I see the trick you play, Lysander. You seem to break away from her as if to escape the fight with me. You coward!"

Lysander works to pry Hermia's fingers from his neck. "Take your cat claws off me! Unstick yourself, you burr! Vile thing, let go!" He raises his fist as if to strike her. Hermia looks straight into his eyes and knows he will let it fall, so she lets him go.

"Why have you grown so mean to me? What change is this that's taken o'er my love?"

"Your love?" he mocks. "It repels and disgusts me. Find another victim to infect…get out of my sight!"

"You jest," she says, recoiling.

"Of course he jests—and so do you," Helena accuses.

"Demetrius, I swear, I'll keep my word and punish thee—" Lysander glares at Demetrius.

"And fight to the death for her?" he looks to Helena. "I don't believe you could."

"What would you have me do then, hurt her?" He puts Hermia in a painful headlock. "Strike her, kill her dead?" He throws her aside. "Although I hate her, I cannot do her harm—"

"What greater harm could ever be than hating me?" Hermia cries. "Hate me? Why? That you would talk this way, my love—am I not Hermia? Are not you Lysander? I am as fair now as I was before. Earlier this night you loved me, yet earlier this night you abandoned me. Why would you have left me—O the gods forbid it being so—am I to take what was our *Yes* has now become your *No*?"

"*Yes*, upon my life, that's so. And never shall desire to see you more. It is hopeless, Hermia, beyond doubt, most certain and true—it is no jest to say I hate thee, for Helena I love, no longer you."

"No," shouts Hermia, "it cannot be!" She fixes Helena with a seething glare. "Deceiving witch, you sorceress, you thief of love! What, have you come by night and stolen my love's heart from him?"

"That you would dare to speak to me so!" cries Helena, drawing herself up to full height. "Have you no modesty, no shame, nor respect for me at all? Forcing cold words like this from off my gentle tongue, and those you spout, to do me wrong—you puppet you!"

"'Puppet'? Yes! That is the way this game does go." She turns on Lysander and Demetrius. "She starts to compare us in stature! She uses her height—her tallness and her height—to prey like this upon you!" Sneering, she turns back to Helena. "And are you now so high in his affection, because I am so dwarfish and so short? How short am I, you painted beanpole? Tell me," she stamps her foot. "How short am I? Too short to rip the eyes from off your face?" And she throws herself with such force at Helena the two of them go staggering back and tumble into the waterfall pool where Hermia, by far the better fighter, takes Helena's head and holds it under water.

"I pray you—" sputters Helena, coming up for a gulp of air. "—Though you mock me—" Hermia submerges her once more, "—let her not kill me, I've done no harm, I've hurt her not!" she cries to Demetrius and Lysander, and exerting all her effort succeeds in tossing Hermia off. "It's not my way to fight—let her not drown me—though you think because she's shorter—"

"Again you call me shorter!" Hermia rails and goes at Helena again, but seeing her chance, the taller girl moves through the pool into deeper water that is well over Hermia's head.

"Good Hermia," Helena raises her voice to be heard above the waterfall behind her, "be not so angry with me. I've always loved you—have always kept your secrets to myself. I've never wronged you once, except that out of love for my Demetrius, I told him you would steal into the wood tonight—that's why I followed after you, and I, for love, then followed after him. But he," she looks to Demetrius, "has cast me off for that, and threatened he would strike me, spurn me, or even kill me too: and now, if you will let me go…to Athens I will make my way, full sorry for my mistakes. I'll bother you no longer. Just please, do let me go: I know how silly and foolish I have been…"

"Go then," Hermia tells her. But Helen doesn't move. "What is holding you back?"

With cautious eyes on Hermia, she walks to the edge of the pool. "—With only a foolish heart to leave behind," she says and lifts herself out of the water.

"With Lysander?" Hermia accuses—storming through the shallows toward her.

"With Demetrius!" Helena replies.

"Be not afraid," Lysander says, "she shall not harm thee more." He hurries over to block Hermia's way.

"No, sir, she will not," assures Demetrius, "though you would take her part."

"When she is angry, she is truly vicious and cruel. She was a very vixen when together we were in school. And though she was but little," Helena taunts, "her temper never matched her size—"

"'Little'?" snaps Hermia. "Nothing but 'short' and 'little'?" She glances over at Lysander. "You will just stand there, and let her insult me like this?" He has hardly finished shrugging when she rushes to go around him, but he grabs her by the arms and holds her back. "I'll hurt you yet!" she rages, punching and kicking her feet in the air as Lysander hoists her off the ground.

"Your hands may be quicker than mine in a fray," teases Helena, "but my legs are longer for running away!" She turns fast, speeds for the forest, and a moment later is swallowed up in the darkness.

"Get you gone," Lysander says scornfully to the still-struggling Hermia. "You tiny thing, you bead, you acorn…you dwarf."

"So hateful and condemning of her who desperately seeks your love?" remarks Demetrius. "Let her alone. Speak not of Helena either. Nor think for one minute that I am fooled by this show of love you've made defending her."

Lysander releases Hermia, who gently puts her arms out to embrace him. He bats them away. "Hermia holds me not," he says to Demetrius, and moves to leave. "Follow me, if you dare."

"Follow? No, I'll go beside you all the way…" And they head off, running after Helena.

Alone and shivering, her clothes soaked through, Hermia gloomily watches them go, then her shoulders begin shaking and she starts to cry. She sobs quietly for several moments…but Oberon, peering out from behind the ferns, takes pity on her hapless situation: he lifts his long-fingered, black-gloved hand, and hurls a bolt of fiery light that surrounds Hermia's body. It pulses briefly, shimmering and bright, then fades away and disappears from sight. She looks down at her clothes in astonishment: her tunic is completely dry.

"I am amazed!" she gasps, "I know not what to say!" But hearing the voices of Lysander and Demetrius calling to Helena in the woods, she hurries from the clearing and enters the forest in an effort to find where they've gone…

Not a minute later, an angry Oberon stalks from the forest holding Puck by one of his pointed ears, his little feet trotting as he tries to keep up.

"Another one of your mistakes!" Oberon rails. "Did you this on purpose to defy me?"

"No, King of Shadows, I misunderstood. Did not you tell me I would know the man, by the Athenian garments he had on? In which respect I did complete my enterprise, by anointing an Athenian's eyes: and so far this night, I'm enjoying what I see— their wrangling is good fun for me."

"Fun, when lovers seek a place to fight? Make haste, Goodfellow! Overcast the night! Blanket the heavens with drooping fog—as black as clouds in Hades be—and lead these testy rivals astray so one comes not within the other's way. Sometimes use Lysander's voice to shout—something Demetrius will be enraged about and sometimes rant as Demetrius would, but keep the one from meeting the other while they wander in the wood—till both the lovers are yearning for sleep, and thoughts give way, and eyes no longer peep. Then crush this herb in Lysander's eye, whose liquor has this certain property, to take away the enchantment of tonight and make him see, on waking, with his usual sight."

"My Fairy Lord, this must be done with haste," says Puck, and he promptly snaps to attention. "The night is passing fast—there's little time to waste—and yonder shines the morning star, at whose approach ghosts near and far, troop home before the rooster's call, to graveyards slouching, one and all. The damned who weren't in churchyards buried, to their wormy beds have scurried, for fear that when the night is gone, the living may look their shame upon. Willfully exiled from day's bright light, their doom is forever to haunt the night."

"But we are spirits of another sort," Oberon contends, "I with the early light of dawn, have oft been known to have my sport, and like a forester the woods may tread, watching the sky all fiery red, and all across the salty sea as sunrise o'er the horizon beams, I turn to blue its vast green streams. But be that as it may, make haste, do not delay— we'll finish this business by break of day!" He shoos Puck to get going then looks at the pool where the waterfall is streaming, where the moon is no longer gleaming…

"Round and round, round and round, I will lead them round and round…" Puck is flying his fastest now, high above the forest: "I am feared in field and town—Goblin, lead them round and round—here comes one now!" He descends through the trees and glides to a stop near the path where Lysander is running along, his sword in his hand, a menacing look on his face.

"Where are you, proud Demetrius? Let me hear your voice!"

"Here I am villain, my sword out and ready!" Puck taunts in the voice of Demetrius. "Where might you be?"

"Closer than you think!" Lysander answers.

"Follow me then to open ground!"

Lysander locates the sound of Puck's voice and charges off in pursuit. But Puck has taken to the air again and soars above the trees…

Soon enough he glances below and casts his eyes on Demetrius. He lowers and lands beside the path, but stays out of view behind a tree and calls the Athenian in Lysander's voice: "You coward, where are you hiding?"

Brandishing his sword, Demetrius looks about. "Speak again, Lysander! You runaway coward, have you fled! Speak! In some bush?" He swings his sword and beats the bushes and jabs the surrounding ferns. "Where are you hiding?"

"Coward yourself!" Puck hails him again, "bragging to the stars and the trees, that you're looking for a fight—well here is one! Come, coward, come and get me!" Puck rustles the leaves right under Demetrius's nose. "I'll whip you with a branch from a sapling tree: but a weakling man would use a sword on thee!"

Demetrius grins, thinking he's found where Lysander is hiding. He creeps slowly forward, raises his sword and lunges hard at some ferns. He glances about. "Not there?"

Puck calls out right behind him: "Follow my voice—you'll never find me here!" With that he streaks into the air and resumes flying over the tops of the trees till he notices Lysander, out of breath and walking slowly along the forest path:

"He runs ahead, keeps luring me on," he complains wearily. "When I come where he calls, then he is gone. The villain is more light-footed than I: I follow fast, yet faster he does fly, and now in the dark I've lost my way." He comes to a stop and looks around. "I'll rest myself here and wait for gentle day." He yawns and sighs then lies down on the path, too tired to find a more suitable spot. "And the moment dawn shows its first gray light, I'll find Demetrius and force him to fight." He rolls on his side, yawns again, and quickly falls asleep.

With a mischievous chuckle, Puck darts back along the path to where Demetrius is flagging as well. "Ho ho ho! Why so scared, coward?" he calls in Lysander's voice. He runs back and forth from bush to bush, giving them a shake as he goes.

"Stop and fight me, if you dare!" Demetrius threatens, "I know you're hiding here somewhere! Come look me in the face! Coward, give up your hiding place!" He charges back and forth on the path but all is silent in the bushes.

"Come closer," Puck pipes up, "I'm right here..."

"No you're not!" He listens for Lysander's voice. "You're mocking me! If ever your face in daylight I see, you'll pay, Lysander, and handsomely. Go your way for now." He sighs and looks around a final time before slumping to the ground. "Tiredness has come over me... For now I'll rest on this cold ground, but morning light shall see you found." Lying half on the path, half off, he closes his eyes and soon is slumbering peacefully—although someone can be heard approaching on the path...

"O wearisome night, O long and tedious night, cut short the hours till morning's light," Helena murmurs quietly to herself. She stops walking and takes a disheartened look around. She looks longingly up at the still-dark sky. "Shine, sunny comforts in the east, so back to Athens I may go at least, away from those who so detest me. Here awhile I'll sleep and rest me…sleep that shuts up sorrow's eye, sleep that helps the tears to dry." She lies herself down on a patch of grass beside the path and within moments has gone to sleep.

Puck, close by, has been watching her. "Yet but three? Come one more. Two of both kinds, makes up four." He peers down the path, a satisfied grin on his impish face when he sees Hermia trudging forward down the way. "Here she comes, all gloomy and sad," he shakes his head in amusement, "—Cupid is a devilish lad, thus to make poor females mad!"

"Never so weary, never so full of woe…covered with the dew…torn by sharp briars. I can no further crawl…no further go. My legs cannot keep pace with my desires. Here will I sink me down till break of day. Heavens shield Lysander, wherever in the woods he makes his way…" Drained of all her energy, she sprawls on the ground and sinks into a deep sleep.

Reveling in the fun, Puck whisks himself back along the path past Helena and Demetrius, "On the ground, sleep sound, sleep sound, on the ground—" until he reaches Lysander. Out with the flower Oberon gave him, to correct his earlier error, he squeezes drops of nectar on the young Athenian's eyes. "When thou wakest…thou will takest…true delight…in thy former lover's sight. In ancient proverbs it is well known: that man and woman should not be alone, in your waking, it shall be shown: Jack shall have Jill, naught shall go ill— henceforward these lovers, can do what they will…."

Into the air once more, Puck hovers above the trees a moment to see that all is as it should be in the Cerean Wood below: four lovers asleep not far from each other, along the forest path. He cheers and utters a gleeful cry, and streaks toward the brightening sky….

Peaseblossom, Mustardseed, Cobweb and Moth spring to life with the other sprites and spirits of Titania's fairy band when their Queen leads her donkey-headed lover, Bottom, from the woods and into a clearing where the rushing brook bends round the trunk of a gray and ancient tree. A look of inner rapture on her face, she ties her emerald-green mask behind her head while Bottom fumbles with the buttons on his pants. Fondling his chest, smothering him in kisses, she takes him by the arm and points him to the white, blue and yellow flowers that blanket the ground beside the forest stream.

"Come sit thee down upon this flowery bed," she says and puts her arms through his, "while I your tender cheeks caress in boundless joy, and wreathe some fragrant garlands round your head, my gentle boy." She bends and picks long strings of colored blossoms, which she drapes around his neck.

"Where's Cobweb?" Bottom asks, sitting down while she works.

"At your service, sir," the little man in cinnamon brown snaps to attention.

"Scratch my head, Cobweb," which Cobweb does. "Where's Moun-*sewer* Peaseblossom?"

"At your service, sir," Peaseblossom in his apple-green suit hurries over.

"Moun-*sewer* Peaseblossom, good moun-*sewer*, get your weapons in hand and kill me a yellow-tipped bumble bee that's resting on top of a purple thistle. And good moun-*sewer*, bring the dung-bucket too." Peaseblossom grimaces. "Someone has to do it—it might as well be you!" Bottom roars with laughter and slaps him on the back, knocking the little man over. He helps Peaseblossom stand up, brushes him off and puts an arm around his little shoulders. "But good Moun-*sewer*, take care the handle doesn't break—I don't want to see you get splattered with dung by mistake!" His uproarious laughter turns into a noisy donkey's bray but no one seems to notice. "Where's Mustardseed then?"

"At your service, sir," the elf in the yellow suit speaks up.

"Give me your fist, moun-*sewer*." Wary because of what happened to the others, he hesitates until frowning Titania motions him to step forward. He bows with an elaborate flourish of his small hand. "No need for courtesies, moun-*sewer*," Bottom assures him.

"What's your will, sir?"

"Nothing, good moun-sewer, except but to help Chevalery Cobweb and scratch all over my head." Mustardseed puts out his fist. Bottom takes it and shows the little man the places to scratch on his mulish head. "I must get to the barber's, moun-sewer, for methinks I am marvelously hairy about the face. And I am such a sensitive ass…at the slightest tickle of my hair, I always need to scratch." Mustardseed nods and squeamishly begins to work on Bottom's itchy head.

"Would you care for some music, my sweet love?" Titania asks, rubbing under his donkey chin.

Bottom considers. "I have a not bad ear for music—let's have the clackers and bells."

The fairies that have come to surround Titania are puzzled by his request.

"—Or perhaps, sweet love, you'd care for something to eat?"

"Why not?" says Bottom, "I could stand a good feed—a bag of your good dried oats," he orders. Methinks I have a great desire for a bale of your best-tasting hay besides—good hay, sweet hay, just the thing to start my day."

"I have an adventurous fairy that shall dig up the squirrel's hoard and fetch the finest nuts, if you desire them," Titania coos.

"I'm not a man for the nuts, my dear. I'd rather have a carrot or two, or maybe a crisp green apple." He opens wide his donkey's mouth and lets out a braying yawn. "But I pray you, in the meantime, let none of your people disturb me. I feel a deposition to sleep coming on."

"Sleep then, and I will fold thee in my arms. Fairies, be gone, away to your employment." In flashes of light the little men and the fairies quickly disperse...

Titania cradles Bottom's head in her lap, adjusting the flower garlands around his head. "Sweet honeysuckle makes a fancy wreath...gardenia will a fragrant scent bequeath. O how I love thee!" she swoons. "How I live for thee!"

Within minutes she too has succumbed to sleep, an arm draped over his chest, her head nuzzled lovingly against his neck...

The branches of the great old elm visible in the moonlight up ahead, Oberon pauses on the wooded path to inspect the work that Puck is supposed to have done. He smiles, pleased: the four young lovers are deep in slumber not far from each other on the forest path. He continues on and arrives at the bend in the brook, Puck perched in the lower branches of the ancient gray tree.

"Welcome good Robin," the Fairy King calls. "See'st thou this pretty sight?" he chuckles.

The two of them peer down at the odd-looking, sleeping couple. "Upon her love-sick rapture I almost look with pity," Oberon admits. "I met her a little while ago within the forest wood, where she roamed and looked for favors for this jackass fool she craves. I upbraided her, then fell to angry argument. When I'd had my fill of taunting, and she, ashamed, with humble words began to beg forgiveness, I came right out and asked her for the orphan Indian child, which she, without ado, agreed to give me on the spot, dispatching some from her fairy band to bear him to my lair in Fairy Land. And now the boy is mine, I'll remove this doting rapture from her eyes. It's time to take the donkey's cap from off the head of this Athenian simpleton as well, that he upon awaking when the others do, they all may back to Athens make their way, and think no more about this night's events, as but the wild confusions of a dream.—But first I will release my Fairy Queen."

He holds out the flower and squeezes some juice in her eyes. "Be what you were formerly, see as you would normally, nectar strong o'er Cupid's flower, work your great transforming power. Now my Titania, wake you, my sweet Queen…"

Her eyes blink open. "Oberon!" She sits up slowly, bewildered, and looks around. "What visions have I seen…I dreamed I was enamored of an ass."

"There lies your love," he points to Bottom, asleep on the ground beside her.

"How came these things to pass?" she cries in disgust, and looks down. "O how mine eyes detest his visage now!"

"We'll talk of it anon. For now there's other business to be done. Robin, remove the ass's head! Titania, call some music forth and let it keep these mortals five," he points to Bottom and the lovers on the path, "in deep and dreamless sleep."

"Music here," Titania calls, "music such as charmeth sleep!" Rising when Oberon offers her his hand, she begins to dance with her black-caped King as elves and fairies spring to life around them, plucking harps and strumming lutes, playing drums and whistling flutes, clapping hands and stamping feet—with such a fervor that the ferns and flowers, the bushes and trees, start swaying to the rhythm of the lively song—even the old gray elm joining in, waving all its branches to the beat of the tune.

Hovering over the sleeping Bottom, Puck prepares to release him from the spell. "When thou wakest up from sleep, once more with your fool's own eyes, you shall begin to peep." He flicks his wrist and waves his hand so a swirling cloud of silver dust twirls around the donkey head, until with a *phht!* Bottom vanishes from sight: a moment later reappearing, asleep in the back of a brown hay-wagon, a donkey hitched to the front.

With a mischievous snicker, Puck slaps it on the rump, and the animal sets off along the wooded path.

"Come, my Queen," Oberon shouts, "we'll celebrate together, you and I, and *rock* the ground whereon these sleepers lie!" He twirls his smiling Queen around the forest floor. "Now you and I are once more friendly, and will tomorrow midnight be, dancing with Theseus triumphantly, blessing him and his Amazon Queen, to long life and prosperity. There shall the Athenian lovers be wed, and taste the pleasures of the marriage bed!"

Amidst the loud commotion, Puck makes a face and cups a hand behind his ear. "Fairy King," he flies over and shouts as Oberon dances on, "attend and mark: is not that, the morning lark?"

Oberon raises his hand and the music abruptly stops. He listens for a moment and, sure enough, the call of the morning lark can be heard. "Then my Queen we'll leave this glade, race to catch the nighttime shades—circle the globe we shall by noon, swifter than the sailing moon."

"Come, my Lord, and in our flight, tell me how it came this night, that I was in the forest found, asleep with mortals on the ground."

They take to the air with their goblins and fairies, and soar away in the brightening sky. Puck flies off too, but hangs back for a look at the four sleeping lovers below. He sighs and shakes his head in amusement—until there comes the sound of hunting horns within the woods. Though he'd like to stay, it's the break of day, which means he must be on his way…

In the faint light of dawn, Theseus, Hippolyta and Egeus are approaching along the forest path with servants and attendants by the dozen, dogs and horses by the score, and a crowd of Athenian citizens and families who have joined the Duke in his wedding-day promenade. After a few moments, Theseus brings the procession to a halt and turns to address the throng.

"Go, one of you, and give our thanks to the forester. For now our promenade is done, yet since it is but early in the day, we'll linger in these woods a little longer. Unleash the hounds, so they can frisk and play." No sooner are they free and bounding back and forth along the path, than Theseus speaks again. "—But wait, what nymphs are slumbering here?"

Egeus sees where he is pointing and rushes forward, perplexed to find his daughter, Hermia, asleep beside the path. "My Lord, this is my daughter!" He glances further down the path and immediately spots the others. "And this Lysander. This Demetrius is, this Helena, old Nedar's daughter Helena—I wonder at their being here together."

"No doubt they rose up early our fair promenade to join—but tell me, Egeus, is not this day the time for Hermia to make her choice?"

"It is, my Lord," Egeus says grimly.

"Go," the Duke calls to a servant, "bid the huntsmen wake these sleepers with their horns." Guards in red and gold uniforms raise their trumpets and sound a signal blast, rousing the lovers from their sleep.

"Good morning friends!" Theseus calls in a friendly voice. "Valentine's day has long gone past. What prompts your wooing now?"

As amazed to see the Duke and his party, as they are by how close they've slept in the night, Hermia, Helena, Demetrius and Lysander get up off the ground and present themselves to Theseus, bowing down before him.

"We beg pardon, my Lord," Lysander speaks first.

"I pray you all stand up," the Duke says kindly, though he turns to the two boys with a questioning frown. "I know you two are rival enemies. How comes this sudden friendship now between you?"

"My Lord, I—I can't explain," Lysander sputters in bewilderment, "but half awake and still but half asleep I seem to be… I cannot truly say how I came here." He glances at the others. "But, as I think—and this I truly do recall, and now as I do think of it believe—I came with Hermia hither. Our plan was to be gone from Athens, to a place where without fear of the city's laws—"

"Enough, my Lord!" Egeus interrupts. "Surely that's all Your Grace need hear—I beg the right of Athenian law—the law upon his guilty head! They would have stolen away by night, Demetrius— would have robbed us of our rights, both you and me: you of a wife, and me of my consent—of my consent that she should be your wife."

"My Lord," Demetrius addresses the Duke, "fair Helen told me of their stealth, of this their plan to escape unto the wood. And I in fury hither followed, fair Helena, out of love, following me. But, my good Lord, I know not by what power—but some power it truly was—my love for Helena melted as the snow. It seemed to me then, like nothing but an idle crush from childhood that had faded so, when with all the faith and virtue in my heart, the object of my love and pure affection, was Helena, only Helena. To her, my Lord, was I betrothed, ere Hermia I ever saw. But as when sick one loathes his food, I now have found my appetite, and wish for her love again: need it, desire it, and long for it, and will forevermore be true to it." He looks to Helena who his words have brought to tears.

Barking as they romp around Theseus, their master, the frisking dogs are eager to get going. Theseus acknowledges a look from his harried attendants, and turns back to finish with Demetrius. "You are fortunate we have found you then," he says, distracted. Demetrius nods, as do the others. "Of your account we will hear more anon. But for now—" He breaks off to pat one of his bigger dogs, and casts his eyes at Egeus, who fumes in red-faced anger. "Egeus," he decrees, "I overrule your protest, for in the temple with Hippolyta and me, these couples shall in eternal union be joined. Away now, let us to Athens, one and all. We'll celebrate with great festivity, the marriage now of loving couples three. Come, Hippolyta…"

And with this pronouncement he leads the procession onward through the forest, the four lovers—falling in behind Theseus and Hippolyta—still reeling from events of the previous night.

"What happened seems so faint and far away," Demetrius admits, "like distant mountains shrouded in morning haze."

"My vision is blurred," Hermia says, "I feel like I'm seeing double."

"The same with me," says Helena lightly, making eyes at Demetrius as she takes him by the arm. "But I have got back my heart's true love, like a jewel I feared was lost but have found again…"

"Is anyone sure that we are awake?" he asks the others. "To me it seems we're yet asleep, still lost in a nighttime dream. Do you think the Duke was actually here, and bid us follow him home?"

"Yes, and my father too," smiles Hermia.

"Oh, *he* was here," Lysander assures her, which draws a chuckle from the others.

"And did the Duke say we'd be married in the temple, together with him and Hippolyta?"

"He did," nods Hermia.

"Then we must be awake after all. Let's go along, and on the way recount our incredible dreams…Methinks I remember a water-fall."

"Methinks I heard a donkey's call," ventures Lysander.

The four of them laugh at such an idea as they move past a wagon at the side of the path with a donkey hitched in front: the very wagon in the back of which, mischievous Puck had placed the sleeping Bottom…

The hunting horns having woken him too, he sits up and hollers at a group of passing Athenians: "When my cue comes, call me at once and I'll say my lines! The next is…" he ponders a moment, "'Most fair Pyramus!'" He looks about and realizes his fellow actors are nowhere to be found. "Peter Quince? Flute? Snout? Starveling? As god's my life, they've deserted me and left me asleep!"

The donkey begins to bray. Bottom gets to his knees and leans forward from behind the driver's seat. "I've had the rarest of dreams," he mutters to the animal, which attracts strange looks from the Athenians walking by—"I've had a dream," he continues, and scratches his head, "past the mind of man to condescend. Puh!" he grunts dismissively, and flops down in the back of the wagon again. "Only an ass would try to explain a dream if he had one such as this. Methought I was—I don't think I can say what. Methought I *was*—methought I *had*—but a man's a blasted fool if he tries to say what it was I was. Eyes have never heard, ears have never seen, hands to taste, tongues to believe, nor the heart to barely describe what this dream of mine was like!" he shouts. A thought strikes him. "I shall get Peter Quince to write a ballad about the dream," he smiles. "He can call it 'Bottom's Dream,' because it has no bottom, or not one you can see." Excited, he grins. "And I'll sing it near the end of the play, when we act before the Duke. Perchance, to make it even more trying, I can sing it when Thisbe is dying!"

Excited now, he climbs up front to the driver's seat, and takes the reins in his hands, snapping them on the donkey's flanks to get the wagon moving. But the animal doesn't budge, which forces Bottom to try again, considerably harder the second time: but still the donkey refuses to move, just blinks and stares ahead. "Giddup!" he snarls in a menacing voice, and lifts the reins, and clicks his tongue—but the moment before he brings down the straps, the wagon lurches and the donkey speeds off, as fast as a donkey can go, with Bottom sprawled in the back of the wagon as it trundles off toward Athens….

Torches being lit along the city street, it is early evening in Athens. Few people are about since the shops and market stalls have been closed for several hours. Flute, Snout, and Starveling are dressed for the play, waiting with Quince by his carpentry shop, gloomy and despondent now that Bottom has disappeared. Props and trunks piled in the street beside them, Flute is trying without much luck to straighten Starveling's pillow breasts, which are sagging now, lop-sided.

"Have you checked at his house to see if he's come home?" Quince asks the others.

"We did so," nods Starveling, "but he's not been heard from, not a peep. Without doubt," he looks solemnly up at the sky, "he's gone to his ever-lasting sleep..."

"If he comes not soon, then the play is ruined: it goes not forward without him, does it?" wonders Flute.

"No it doesn't," Quince broods. "There's not a man in Athens who could play the part of Pyramus better than he."

"'Tis true," Flute agrees. "Bottom has the cleanest intelligence of any craftsman in all the city."

"—And capturing presence too," Quince points out. "And he's a very paramour when it comes to his sweet-sounding voice."

"Methinks you must mean 'paragon,'" says Flute. "A paramour is, God bless us, a dirty thing to be." A ribald grin, he pokes Starveling between the legs and they laugh, not noticing Snug has come running up with news.

"Masters, the Duke is returned to his palace with the young lords and ladies who will be married together with him and his Amazon Queen. If only Pyramus Bottom could have played...all our fortunes would have been made."

"Good old Bottom!" cries Flute, and his eyes brim up with tears, Starveling as well beginning to weep—when suddenly a voice rings out in the street:

"Pyramus, masters, come from Ninny's tomb!!"

Not only is Bottom and alive and well, he's barreling toward his cheering friends at the reins of the donkey wagon! He pulls it to a stop by the carpentry shop, climbs quickly down and basks in the embraces and back-slapping hugs of Quince and his fellow craftsmen. "Where are these lads? Where are these stout-hearted men?" he swaggers.

"O glorious day! O happy hour!" Quince rejoices.

"Are we saved Peter Quince?" asks Flute.

"That we are, my boy!"

"Masters," Bottom says and settles the company down. "I could tell you the most wondrous but startling tale, but ask me not now. For if I did, as I am a true Athenian, you'd hoot and holler and call me a liar, and none would ever believe me."

"Let us hear it, good Bottom," Quince pleads, intrigued.

The others chorus in—they want to hear too—but Bottom shakes his head and refuses. "You'll not get a word out of me, good masters." The others groan, disappointed. "What I *will* tell you all, is this: the Duke is done his dinner. If we get our things together quick, look over our parts, make sure we are set, and construct ourselves to the palace at once, why, the long and short of the story is, that our play has been recommended!"

After more cheering and embracing, Quince goes into action giving orders for the props and trunks to be lifted on board the donkey wagon.

While the others work, Bottom looks on, giving pointers they will need to remember. "Thisbe, make sure your hair is straight, and Thisbe's mother," he winks at Starveling's uneven breasts, "make sure that yours are too! Whoever plays the lion's part, don't cut your nails, for they will be your fearsome claws! And actors all, leave onions and garlic for now, for the words we mutter require sweet breath—to be spoken as sweet as ever could be!" He clambers into the wagon seat and Starveling hands him the reins. "And this being so, no doubt our faithful audience will say, '*Pyramus and Thisbe* is a right fine play!' But no more words, away!!"

He snaps the reins, the others shout, the donkey strains, and the overloaded wagon slowly begins to move out....

Along with the nobles and high-ranking city officials, Theseus has invited citizens from all walks of life to be present at the celebration he is giving tonight in honor of his marriage to Hippolyta, the crowd so large in the palace courtyard that scaffolds have been constructed along the torch-lit walls so all can see forward to the stage: a raised wooden platform slightly higher in the back than at the front, enclosed on three sides by dark blue curtains draped from tall golden poles where banners flying the Duke's red-and-gold crest are waving in the light evening breeze.

There is a hush in the air as Hippolyta's young archers are about to conclude their demonstration. A catapult has been made ready off to one side of the stage, set for shooting two gold balls, which have been placed in the holder at the end of the firing arm. The nine girls stand with their backs to the audience, just in front of Theseus and Hippolyta, who are sitting in the center of the front row. He stops talking to a gentleman behind him when Hippolyta draws his attention to the archers who are waiting for him so they can begin. The Duke turns around in his seat and nods to the girls that he is ready.

A servant speaks to the first two girls then signals to the servant manning the catapult. He presses the release and the catapult arm shoots the two gold balls high into the air over the stage. The girls let go their arrows, which fly at the soaring balls, striking them so they shatter and two streams of shimmering gold confetti rain down. The audience applauds, the two girls bow. When three more pairs have repeated the demonstration—the gold balls smaller each time—the ninth and final archer takes her place. She bows nervously to Theseus and Hippolyta, who offers a confidence-boosting smile, then turns and readies her arrow in the bow. The catapult fires and this time the gold ball is no bigger than an orange. Moving with the target, the young girl eyes the gold ball and lets go…striking it precisely so it bursts open like the others—but this time a white feather floats to the ground with something small attached to the bottom. While applause for the young girl's performance fills the air, a servant waits for the falling feather to land and picks it up. He runs it over to the young archer and hands it to her. She gasps: it's a solid gold arrowhead. Turning to Theseus, she bows in appreciation, waves to the audience who are still clapping for her, and leaves to take her seat.

With something on her mind, Hippolyta turns to the Duke. "'Tis strange, my Theseus, what these lovers speak of…"

"More strange than true," he answers casually. "I've never believed in old fables or fairy tales. Lovers and madmen have such raving minds, such wild imaginations to dream up stories common reason may in no way comprehend. The lunatic, the lover, and the poet are in imagination all the same in my opinion: one believes the earth teems with more devils than hell can hold. That's the madman. The lover, no less crazed, sees beauty as little more than the features of his beloved's face. The poet, in passionate frenzy, glances from heaven to earth, earth to heaven, and as imagination gives shape and form to ideas being born, the poet's pen then brings them to life, giving to airy nothing, both substance and a name. Such tricks can the imagination play, that it makes things appear which are not really there—as at night when we receive a scare, and see a bush we have mistaken for a bear."

"But the stories of the night they told, differed not in detail whatsoever," she points out. "It seems they witnessed with their eyes what dreams and fancies could never devise."

"Here come the lovers now, joyfully restored," Theseus says by way of an answer: Hermia and Lysander, Helena and Demetrius are making their way to their seats on either side of Theseus and Hippolyta.

"Join us, gentle friends," Theseus greets them, and may your days be happy and loving."

"And may yours even moreso be," offers Lysander. He bows and takes up his seat next to Hippolyta.

"Come now," calls Theseus, "what plays, what dances, what entertainments are there in store to help us pass these hours after supper and before bed? Where is my usual manager of mirth?"

Flustered and irritable, Philostrate has been attending to a matter over by the stage where the various acting troupes are waiting to hear if they will be called upon to perform: the voluptuous drunken women with their inch-long fingernails, the white-bearded old man with the yellow-gowned dancers who are braiding ribbons in each other's hair, the bearded and well muscled men in loin-cloths who will breathe fire at the man with the lyre, whose magnificent hair was burned by accident during rehearsal. Tonight he is again sporting a magnificent head of hair, however it's a woman's blonde wig, and he is hoping no-one will notice.

But standing with Quince and the others, Bottom has borrowed Starveling's chimney-sweeping broom and used the handle to nudge the lyre player's wig so it slips to one side. Livid, he wheels quickly to see who the culprit is, but Bottom has stepped back behind Starveling and looks on with an air of perfect innocence, while Starveling waves his breasts in the lyre-player's face then grimaces and sticks out his tongue.

"Here, mighty Theseus," Philostrate rushes up, puffing and out of breath as he presents himself to the Duke.

"Well now," says Theseus, "what pastimes and diversions are arranged for us tonight? What dancers and musicians will our eyes and ears delight?"

It suddenly occurs to Philostrate that he's forgotten the paper where the night's plays are listed. He thinks quickly and manages to answer the Duke without missing more than a few beats: "Here be the entertainments that are prepared, my Lord. Make choice of which your Highness will see first." He clears his throat importantly and begins. "The attack of the fire-breathing eunuchs at Thrace."

Theseus shakes his head. "That is an old chestnut. Besides, it was played after I slew the minotaur at Crete."

Philostrate continues. "The death of Orpheus at the hands of the drunken wom—"

"No no," the Duke cuts him off. "They performed this at the wedding of my cousin Hercules and a riot broke out in which the bride herself was injured."

"Socrates and the three Muses mourning the death of learning."

"Much too serious and philosophical, not in keeping with nuptial festivities."

A servant has run up and handed Philostrate the list of plays. He finds his place and reads. "'A tedious but brief scene of young Pyramus and his love Thisbe…very tragical mirth'?" he raises his voice as a question.

"'Merry and tragic'?" the Duke asks. " 'Tedious and brief'? That would be like hot ice, or black snow! How could I find something that sounds so disagreeable agreeing with me? Tell me more," the Duke says, intrigued.

"Well," Philostrate says uncomfortably, "it's a play, my Lord, some ten words long, which is as brief as I have known a play to be, but by ten words, my Lord, I find even then it is too long, which is what makes it tedious. For in the entire play there is not one word worth hearing, not one actor fitted for his part. And tragic it is, my noble Lord, for Pyramus at the end doth kill himself, which, when I saw it rehearsed, I must confess it brought me to tears, but these were merry tears, my Lord, the kind loud laughter sheds." He smirks, satisfied that his description has been disparaging enough to put Theseus off.

But to Philostrate's chagrin, Theseus is more curious than ever. "Who are they that do perform it?" he asks.

"Laboring men who work here in Athens—but never labored with their minds until now, and now have overtaxed their already limited if not feeble memories preparing this play," he says maliciously, "though to their credit they *have* prepared it in time for the royal wedding day."

"We will hear that," Theseus decides.

Philostrate panics. "No, my noble Lord," he says in an attempt to dissuade the Duke, "it is not for you, believe me!"

"I have seen some of it myself," Egeus pipes up from his seat near Theseus. "It is nothing, my Lord, nothing at all."

"Unless it be your pleasure to see fools take a most tragic play and make of it a mockery."

"I will see that play," Theseus repeats, "for how could anything be amiss, if done in devotion, pride and duty, and a spirit of genuine simpleness? Bring them forward for our pleasure."

Philostrate bows and reluctantly heads back toward the stage area to inform Quince and his cast that the Duke has selected them to perform their *Pyramus and Thisbe*.

Hippolyta leans over to Theseus. "I hate to see simple folk mocked for the amusement of their betters."

"You shall see no such thing, my love," he assures her.

"But he says they know nothing about what they do."

"The kinder are we, then, to applaud them when they're through. Respect will be paid to the effort they've made, and the pleasure they take in what they do. Tongue-tied simplicity and clumsy moving, prompt me not to be disapproving. In my experience, the audience is won by the feeling with which a play is done."

"So please Your Grace, the actors are ready," Philostrate calls to the Duke.

"Let them begin!"

Receiving their signal, the heralds raise their long brass trumpets and sound an opening fanfare, during which Quince goes to Philostrate, gestures at the torches surrounding the stage then points up at the full moon in the sky. Philostrate frowns and shakes his head *No*, but Quince persists until Philostrate relents and sends a party of servants to extinguish the torches on the stage, the audience chattering in curious anticipation as light from the moon casts the stage in a soft and enchanting blue light.

Quince comes forward and bows to the crowd.

"If we offend, it is with our good will. That you should think, we come not to offend, may it please you to think we only do so with our good will. To show our simple skill, that is the true beginning of our end. Consider then, we come but in despite. We do not come, in hopes we will content you, our true intent is. All for your delight. We are not here that, after, you will repent you. Having watched. The actors are at hand, and by their show, you shall know all. That you are likely to know."

Amused by Quince's choppy deliver, the crowd stirs but waits patiently as the actors appear on stage and take up positions behind him: Bottom and Flute as Pyramus and Thisbe in the center, Snout as The Wall between them, Starveling off to one side as Moonshine, and Snug as The Lion.

"People," Quince continues, "perchance you wonder at this show." He steps back, moving toward his actors as he speaks. "But wonder on, till truth make all things plain. This man," he sets his hand on Bottom's shoulder, "is Pyramus, if you would like to know. This beauteous lady," he shifts over and puts his hand on Flute, "Thisbe, who he loves and who, you can be certain, loves him too.

"This man," he crosses to Snout, "with lime and plaster cast, presents The Wall, that vile Wall which kept these lovers apart." He has to wait while Snout holds up his white piece of cast plaster with a small hole in its center. When some in the audience laugh he lifts it higher—until Quince clears his throat, and he quickly lowers it. "—And through Wall's chink, poor souls—" Snout pokes his finger through the hole at the mention of 'chink', "—they are content to whisper. At which let no man wonder..." his voice trails off as though he might have forgotten his line.

"This man," he comes up to Starveling, "with lantern, dog and chimney-sweeping broom, presenteth Moonshine." He asks urgently under his breath, about the dog, Starveling making a guilty face: he seems to have forgotten, but to make up for the omission he thrusts the bristle-end of the broom over his head with one hand, and puts the burning lantern behind it with the other: a moonlight-through-the-trees effect.

"For if you didn't know," Quince carries on, "by moonshine did these lovers find it safe to meet at Ninus's Tomb, and there, there, to woo." He approaches Snug who is crouched on all fours, with a rolled-up, pale-red blanket encircling his head, three cat whiskers drawn in charcoal on his cheeks. "This grisly beast—" Snug lifts his head and roars not loud, but long, "which Lion has the name, the trusty Thisbe, coming first by night, did scare away, or rather did affright. And as she fled, her mantle she let go," Flute takes the white linen mantle from around his shoulders and lets it fall, "which Lion vile, with bloody mouth did stain." Snug bounds over on all fours, picks up the mantle in his teeth and shakes it savagely back and forth for a moment before dropping it and pouncing his way off stage.

"Along comes Pyramus, sweet youth and tall," Quince says feelingly, Bottom strolling across the stage then stopping when he spots the fallen mantle which Snug has left behind, "—yes, Pyramus finds his trusty Thisbe's mantle slain." Bottom picks up the mantle and holds it, grief-stricken, against his cheek. "Whereat with blade, with bloody blameful blade, he bravely struck his boiling bloody breast," Bottom makes as if to stab himself with a crooked prop sword he's made, "while Thisbe, tarrying near in mulberry shade, came running forth, his dagger drew on herself, and died. As for the rest." He pauses and looks to the others and gestures with his hand, "Let Lion, Moonshine, Wall and our lovers twain, tell more of the story while here," he points to the stage, "they do remain." He walks off and slips behind the curtain.

Snout steps forward with his piece of white cast plaster. "In this same interlude it doth befall, that I, one Snout by name, present a wall, and such a wall as I would have you think, that had in it a crannied hole, or chink, through which the lovers Pyramus and Thisbe, did whisper often, very secretly. This lime, this plaster cast are meant to show, that I am that same wall, the truth is so: and this the cranny is," he inserts his finger and wiggles it, "right and sinister, through which the fearful lovers are to whisper."

Bottom, playing Pyramus, comes walking and stands face to face with Snout, the plaster cast between them. "O grim-faced night," he gazes at the sky, "O night with hue so black! O night, which ever art when day is not! O night, O night, alack, alack, I fear my Thisbe's promise is forgot! And thou," he drops to his knees and reaches out his hands, "O wall, O sweet, O lovely wall," he runs his hands over the plaster, "that stand'st between her father's ground and mine, thou wall, O wall, O sweet and lovely wall, show me thy chink, to blink through with my eyne." Snout lifts the plaster so the hole is level with the kneeling Bottom's head. "Thanks, courteous wall: Jove shield thee well for this," and he puts his eye close and peers through the hole. "But what see I? No Thisbe do I see, O my, O me. O wicked wall, through whom I see no bliss, cursed be your stones for thus deceiving me!"

"The wall being able to speak," someone calls out, "perhaps he'll curse you back!" The comment sets off scattered applause and other jokes within the crowd.

"No, in truth sir, he would not," Bottom breaks character and answers the heckler, "'Deceiving me' is Thisbe's cue to enter, and I am to spy her through the wall. You shall see it happen as soon as—but yonder she comes…"

As Thisbe, Flute enters and comes to stand in front of Snout, who has turned around so he's facing her, Bottom still on his knees, now looking into Snout's behind. Thisbe kneels down, raises her hands and touches them to the wall, her mouth in front of the hole, which is level with Snout's crotch. She begins to speak. "O wall, full often hast thou heard my moans, for parting my fair Pyramus and me! My cherry lips have often kissed thy stones," Snout looks down, trying not to laugh, "thy stones with lime and plaster covered over."

"I see a voice!" cries Bottom from behind Snout. "Now will I to the chink, to spy and hear my Thisbe's face. This-beee?" he calls, drawing out the last syllable so Snout will be reminded to turn around. When Snout for some reason doesn't budge, Bottom takes a finger and pokes him in the rear. Snout jumps and kicks back with his heel, catching Bottom between the legs."

The audience laughter, which has been increasing in the last several minutes, edges now toward hysterics.

"My love thou art," swoons Thisbe, "my love you are I think," she frowns, confused by the rampant laughter.

Snout turns so Bottom can speak.

"Think what thou wilt, I am thy lover dear, and behold! Behold me through this chink."

"O lover true!" cries Thisbe to Snout's behind. He moves to turn but Pyramus has taken hold of the plaster to keep him where he is.

"O lover do!" Bottom calls to Thisbe through the hole, "O, kiss me through the hole in this vile wall!" and he lets go of the plaster so Snout can finally turn.

"I kiss the wall's hole," Thisbe protests as soon as she can get her mouth to the hole, "not your lips at all."

Snout wheels around for Bottom.

"Wilt thou at Ninny's Tomb meet me straight away?"

Back to Thisbe goes Snout, growing flustered.

"Come life, come death, I'll meet you without delay."

To Snout's relief, they get to their feet and depart in different directions. He turns to face the audience. "Thus have I, The Wall, my part acquitted so. And being done, thus Wall away doth go." He retreats behind the curtain at the side as Snug and Starveling, playing Lion and Moonshine, hurry forward and take their places.

Snug goes first. "You ladies, you whose gentle hearts do fear the smallest monstrous mouse that creeps on floor, may now, perchance, both quake and tremble here, when lion rough in wildest rage doth roar, but know that I, Snug the woodworker am that lion fell and fierce, and if I should as Lion come to strife, it were a pity, on my very life."

Starveling's turn, he hoists his broom by the handle and holds the lantern up behind.

"Moonshine is the part I play, but also Thisbe's mother." She lowers the broom and lantern, and curtsies. I keep the villain Pyramus, from my sweet young daughter away!" She lifts the lantern and broom again. "This lantern doth the shining moon present...myself the Man in the Moon do seem to be," he smiles good-naturedly at his joke, but, distracted, struggles for an awkward moment, unable to remember his line...so he breaks from character, looks to the audience and explains. "All that I have to say is, to tell you that the lantern is the moon, I the Man in the Moon, this chimney brush my own chimney brush –"

But Thisbe cuts him off as she crosses the stage. "This is old Ninny's Tomb." She looks desperately around. "But where is my lord?"

"Orrrrr!" Lion roars.

Thisbe puts a hand up to her frightened face and flees, the mantle she wears on her shoulders flying off and floating to the ground behind her, where Lion picks it up in his teeth and shakes it fiercely back and forth. In a moment he spits it out and leaves.

Quince shoving him forward from the side curtains, Bottom presents himself and kneels beneath Moonshine's lantern and broom.

"Sweet Moon, I thank thee for thy sunny beams," he moves his head to one side so he can see over her protruding bosoms to the lantern light, but his face remains in shadow. "I *thank* thee moon for shining now so bright," he says and leans the other way, but his face is still in darkness. "For by thy gracious, golden, glittering *gleams*," he growls impatiently, I hope to take of truest Thisbe sight. But wait! O spite!" He spots the mantle Lion chewed, and crawls over on his knees to pick it up. The garment is spotted with what looks like blood. "But mark, poor knight, what dreadful grief is here? Eyes, do you *see*? How can it *be*? O dainty duck! O dear! Thy mantle good—What! Stained with blood? Approach ye Furies evil. O Fates, come, come! Put an end to my life: conquer, crush, conclude, and kill.

"O wherefore, Nature, did you ever lions frame," he cries, "since lion vile hath just deflowered my dear? Which is—no, no—which was the fairest dame, that ever lived, that loved, that liked, that looked with cheer. Come my tears, confound! Out sword, and wound the breast of Pyramus," he draws his makeshift sword and holds it with two hands on the handle, the crooked blade pointing away from his chest so he quickly bends it back, though when it won't stay he proceeds anyway. "Ay, that left breast," he shifts the sword to the other side, "where the heart doth rest," and he bends over, the sword appearing to plunge into his stomach. "Thus die I," he croaks, "thus, thus, thus!" He lies still. "Now I am dead, now I am fled," he moans. "My soul is in the sky: tongue lose thy light, Moon, take thy flight!" Moonshine, her pillow breasts bouncing, leaves the stage.

Bottom shoots up suddenly into a sitting position. "Now die, die, die, die, die." He falls back down, makes his body shudder and shake, forces his legs to tremble, and finally stops moving.

Thisbe returns to the stage and creeps cautiously over. "Asleep, my love?" She gets down and checks his body. "What, dead my love?" She cradles his head in her arms. "O Pyramus, arise! Speak! Speak! Quite dumb?" She slaps his face—Bottom winces and bats her hand away as she moves to do it again. "Dead, dead? A tomb must cover thy sweet eyes now. These lily lips, this cherry nose, these yellow buttercup cheeks, are gone, are gone! Lovers, let out your moans…" She spots his weapon. "Come, trusty sword, come blade, my breast invade!" She stabs herself with the flimsy sword and sprawls across Bottom with unexpected force: he angrily pushes her off—she rolls over and away. "Farewell friends! Thus Thisbe ends!" She raises herself up on one hand, "Adieu, adieu, adieu!" then she collapses and gradually lies still.

The audience, unsure if the play is over, stays silent and continues watching the stage.

"The End!" a voice finally shouts from behind the curtains, and wild applause begins: people are cheering and whistling and shouting for the actors to take their bows, which they happily do. The trumpets blare and music fills the air. Servants rush forward and give flower bouquets to Moonshine and Thisbe, who curtsy awkwardly and bow, Pyramus joins hands with Quince and Snout, and Snug the Lion runs about, sounding his mighty roar—but everything suddenly comes to a stop. Everyone present stands motionless, frozen, still...

Puck appears out of nowhere and walks forward between the frozen actors to stand at the front of the stage.

"If we shadows have offended, think but this, and all is mended: that you have but slumbered here, while these visions did appear. Our story might be over friends, but whether it is, on you depends. A dream, you say? Perhaps. May be. Time will tell, and we shall see. For now, good night. For now, good luck. For now farewell, from honest Puck.

Then with a blink, he disappears....

New Directions

The Young and the Restless: *Change*
The Human Season: *Time and Nature*
Eyes Wide Shut: *Vision and Blindness*
Cosmos: *The Light and The Dark*
Nothing But: *The Truth in Shakespeare*
Relationscripts: *Characters as People*
Idol Gossip: *Rumours and Realities*
Wherefore?? *The Why in Shakespeare*
Upstage, Downstage: *The Play's the Thing*
Being There: *Exteriors and Interiors*
Dangerous Liaisons: *Love, Lust and Passion*
Iambic Rap: *Shakespeare's Words*
P.D.Q.: *Problems, Decisions, Quandaries*
Antic Dispositions: *Roles and Masks*
The View From Here: *Public vs. Private Parts*
3D: *Dreams, Destiny, Desires*
Mind Games: *The Social Seen*
Vox: *The Voice of Reason*

The Shakespeare Novels

Hamlet
King Lear
Macbeth
Midsummer Night's Dream
Othello
Romeo and Juliet
Twelfth Night

www.crebermonde.com

Shakespeare Manga Novels

Fall 2007

Midsummer Night's Dream
Macbeth
King Lear
Romeo and Juliet
Othello
Hamlet

www.shakespearemanga.com

Paul Illidge is a novelist and screenwriter who taught high school English for many years. He is the creator of *Shakespeare Manga*, the plays in graphic novel format, and author of the forthcoming *Shakespeare and I*. He is currently working on *Shakespeare in America*, a feature-film documentary. Paul Illidge lives with his three children beside the Rouge River in eastern Toronto.